Fear and Honor
(The Lightwood Affair Book 2)

By M. S. Parker

This book is a work of fiction. The names, characters, places and incidents are products of the writer's imagination or have been used fictitiously and are not to be construed as real. Any resemblance to persons, living or dead, actual events, locales or organizations is entirely coincidental.
Copyright © 2016 Belmonte Publishing
Published by Belmonte Publishing.

ISBN-13: 978-1541364776

ISBN-10: 1541364775

Table of Contents

Chapter 1 1
Chapter 2 9
Chapter 3 17
Chapter 4 27
Chapter 5 37
Chapter 6 45
Chapter 7 53
Chapter 8 67
Chapter 9 75
Chapter 10 91
Chapter 11 97
Chapter 12 105
Chapter 13 113
Chapter 14 123
Chapter 15 133
Chapter 16 141
Chapter 17 151
Chapter 18 157
Chapter 19 171
Chapter 20 179
Chapter 21 187
Chapter 22 193
Chapter 23 199

Chapter 24	205
Chapter 25	211
Chapter 26	217
Chapter 27	221
Chapter 28	229
Chapter 29	237
Chapter 30	247
More from M.S. Parker	254
Acknowledgement	255
About the Author	256

Chapter 1

"Are you ready?"

I looked up at my husband and gave him a weak smile as I pulled on my dress. I'd woken up this morning with a strong feeling of dread, a stirring inside that set me on edge. I'd enjoyed the makeshift honeymoon and appreciated the time I spent with Gracen. It had definitely helped us adjust to the situation before we had to head back to the Lightwood estate. But I still felt like there would never be enough time to adapt to the circumstances we'd been flung into.

Then again, considering I'd been born in 1986 and today was July 7, 1775, I wasn't sure if any amount of time would ever be enough. I'd served in the United States Army, and now I was living in and experiencing a time and place where that army didn't even exist. I still didn't know how a car accident on my way to my parents' house outside of Boston had transported me more than two hundred years into the past, or if whatever had done it would take me back.

And as I looked over at the man I married just a few days ago, I knew that I truly didn't want to go back to my own time. I loved my parents and my brother, the men in my unit, but Gracen Lightwood had quickly become my world. I'd never believed in love at first sight, or even second or third sight, but I'd also never believed in time travel either, so the past couple of weeks had been quite the eye-opener.

Strong arms slid around my waist and pulled me back against a lean, hard body.

"You will be fine," Gracen whispered, his breath caressing my ear. I didn't have to look up at him to know the exact shade of his emerald eyes, of his raven-black waves. To know every line of his face and body.

"I wish I was as sure as you are," I muttered as I put my hands over his. I wasn't only worried about me though. Once we returned to the Lightwood estate, Gracen would be at the mercy of his father, and I knew that our new, unannounced marriage wouldn't make things any easier for him.

Roston Lightwood was going to shit a brick when he found out what Gracen and I had done.

"It's time to head back." Gracen shifted and took my hand in his. "No matter what happens, we're in this together."

I nodded and mustered the best smile I could. This wouldn't be easy, and not only because of the revolution ahead. The Lightwoods were well-known Loyalists, and Gracen's father wanted his only son to join the British army to uphold the integrity of the family name. Gracen and I weren't only going back into an awkward situation. It was a dangerous one.

Knowing that didn't push me into talking him out of it though, and I still let him lead me outside to where a carriage was waiting for us. I scowled at my skirts as I climbed inside, wishing I could dress in the uniform I'd arrived in, but that wouldn't exactly be a good idea, not if I wanted to blend in. I loved my new husband, but I didn't love the eighteenth-century clothes.

I leaned against Gracen as the carriage started to move and tried not to think about anything other than him and the time we spent together over the past couple of days. Pleasant memories to steel me against what was to come.

We made good time and arrived back at the estate a little after mid-day. Part of me had hoped for a few delays along the way, but there'd been nothing to spare us from the inevitable encounter with Roston. Only the silence between Gracen and I as we mentally braced ourselves for the welcome we were sure to receive.

Titus, the steward of the house, was the first to notice our arrival when Gracen walked into the estate, and he wasn't pleased to see me.

"Welcome back, Master Gracen." Titus spoke to my husband, but his dark eyes were trained on me, the sheer disgust and contempt clear.

Titus had hated me from the first moment he'd seen me, and judging by the way his mouth twisted into a scowl when he saw Gracen's hand wrapped around mine, that loathing had only gotten worse.

"Where's my father?" Gracen asked with barely a look in the steward's direction.

"The library, I believe, Master Gracen." Titus's tone said he didn't like being put in his place, even though his face was carefully blank.

I followed Gracen without a backward glance. My stomach was in knots, but I refused to show it. We were already married, and as far as I knew, there'd be no getting around it without a scandal. It definitely wasn't like the time I was from. While arranged marriages weren't quite as commonplace as they had been in the past, there was definitely a stigma to marrying outside rank, and those in the higher class were strongly encouraged to follow their parents' suggestions when it came to choosing a spouse. Gracen deciding to marry a girl who'd been a kitchen maid only a short while ago would shock the whole of society.

He led me down the hall I'd swept, dusted, and scrubbed numerous times over the past few weeks, and the surreal feeling surrounding me grew with every step. Even though enough had happened to prove to me that this was indeed my life at the moment, it still felt like some sort of strange dream.

My husband didn't bother knocking on the heavy oak door, but pushed it open, striding in with his hand still firmly wrapped around mine, despite knowing how his father felt about me. In that instant, my love for him flared bright and hot, reminding me of why I'd chosen to remain here instead of seeking a way back to my time.

Roston Lightwood sat behind his colossal desk, a Loyalist friend of his seated on the other side, but when we entered, the elder Lightwood shot to his feet, myriad expressions crossing his face, one right after the other – none of them pleasant. His eyes darted from his son's face to our intertwined hands, hatred and embarrassment mingled in his glare. It was obvious that our expectations of his reaction had been entirely too accurate. The man was already fuming, and we hadn't said a word. Roston's visitor stayed where he was, looking back and forth between Roston and Gracen, as if the entire thing was an amusing spectacle. Based on the other friends of Roston's I'd met, I didn't doubt for one second that he was hoping for something to gossip about.

Roston's cold hazel eyes once more slid down to where Gracen's hand was linked with mine, and a muscle in his jaw tightened. "I trust you have an explanation for this." His voice was steel.

"Good evening to you too, Father," Gracen responded coolly.

"For heaven's sake, disentangle yourself from that servant girl right this moment." Roston gave a quick glance to his friend. "Have you no decency? I'll not have you bringing disgrace to our family name by flaunting something so...unseemly."

Gracen raised his chin slightly. "I believe we have quite different opinions as to what disgraces a family name."

Roston's face went white, but I doubted it was from anything other than fury. He turned to his friend. "If you'll excuse us, I have a family matter which needs attending. Shall we continue our discussion at a later time?"

"Of course," the visitor replied, barely hiding his glee at the altercation. He stood and allowed Roston to lead him to the door.

After instructing Titus to walk their guest out, Roston closed the door and turned on us. "Did you abandon your post for *her*? Have you any idea the penalty for such actions?"

"I never enlisted."

Roston's face was slowly turning into a light shade of red, and his hands curled into fists. Without an audience, he made no attempt to rein in his temper. "Then you're worse than a deserter. You're a coward."

My nails dug into my palm as I made a fist of my own. I'd kept my mouth shut and my head down when I was a servant here, but I'd done it mostly to avoid putting Gracen in danger. My patience, however, only stretched so far, and it was reaching its breaking point. Gracen's hand tightened on mine, as if he could sense that I was close to snapping.

"As for you," Roston turned to me, "you're no longer welcome in this house."

Gracen responded before I could. "We will leave at first light then."

Color filled Roston's face so suddenly that the medic in me wondered about his blood pressure. "Titus will show this *girl* to the door, while you and I have a conversation regarding where your loyalties should lie. I will not have my only son chasing after a servant—"

"Honor is my wife."

The silence was suddenly deafening, stretching out between us. I held my breath as I waited for what was to come.

Roston crossed the distance between us in only a few long strides, grabbing the front of Gracen's shirt and pulling us apart as he shoved Gracen back a few steps.

"Stop it!" I yelled as Gracen's hand was ripped from mine.

They both ignored me as Gracen set his feet and brought them to a halt.

"How could you be this foolish?!" Roston's voice was low and dangerous. "We have a reputation and a family name to uphold! You may bed a servant if you wish, but you do not *marry* them! Your selfish actions may have very well ruined us!"

I reminded myself to let my husband respond. Not because he was a man and it was his place, but because this was his father which made it his right. He took a step to the side, his gaze locked on his father until Roston released the front of his shirt.

"I am my own man, Father." Gracen's voice was stiff. "I know you have always wished that I followed more closely in your footsteps, but I will not fight a war I do not believe in." He held out his hand for me, and I took it. "I love Honor, and I have married her. I do not regret it, and I will not apologize for it."

Roston's hand cracked against the side of Gracen's face, the sound echoing in the momentary silence.

"You bastard!" I snapped as I took a step forward.

As soon as the words left my mouth, Roston swung his hand toward me. Before I could make a move to defend myself, Gracen put himself between me and the blow. He didn't even flinch as the backhand slap meant for me caught the side of his neck, Roston's ring leaving a jagged cut across his skin. Blood welled instantly, the crimson stark against Gracen's tanned skin.

"Get out. Now."

Chapter 2

I slowly seated myself on the bed next to Gracen, dipping a rag into a mixture of warm water and witch hazel so I wouldn't have to look at him just yet. I was having a hard enough time keeping my hands from shaking as I wrung excess water from the rag. I took a slow, steadying breath and pressed the rag against his neck. He sucked in air through his teeth, squeezing his eyes shut as I wiped the blood from around the wound. I couldn't even look at the red handprint on his cheek. I'd dealt with injuries exponentially worse than this, but those hadn't been my husband. Or my fault.

"Gracen, I'm so sorry," I whispered around the lump in my throat. "So, so sorry."

"You are not to blame, my love." He wrapped his fingers around mine and raised our hands to press his lips against my knuckles.

"Yes, I am." I swallowed hard. "If I hadn't come here, if you hadn't found me and brought me home..." I trailed off.

"Then I would have been lost," he said firmly, eyes blazing. "You coming into my life gave me the courage to stand up to my father. To do what is right. You gave me a reason to fight."

I blinked back the tears that burned against my eyelids. I lifted our hands, pressed my lips against his palm. "How could he do that to you? You're his son," I whispered.

"He's a hard man," Gracen replied. "Some of the servants say that things were different before my mother died, but I was too young to remember." He kissed the top of my head. "Besides, this is nothing. You should have seen the beating I received when he caught me feeding my dinner to the dog when I was a young boy. Such a thrashing that I couldn't sit for three days."

I jerked back and glared up at him. "That's not funny, Gracen."

He gave me a wry smile. "It didn't feel that way at the time either."

I started to get up, but he grasped my arm and pulled me down next to him again, a puzzled expression on his face.

"Did I say something wrong?" He reached up to tuck a strand of chestnut brown hair behind my ear.

"Child abuse isn't something to joke about." Images flashed through my mind, memories of a friend I'd had as a child. A little girl who'd come to school with black eyes half a dozen times before I'd finally broken my promise to stay quiet and told my father.

"Child abuse?" Gracen's forehead furrowed in confusion. "I don't understand."

Of course he didn't. This was the eighteenth century. Using hands and fists, belts, and whatever else came to hand, to discipline a child or servant – or hell, even a wife – wasn't only seen as a normal and everyday course of action, it was expected. Unless it resulted in some sort of permanent damage, no one blinked.

I laced my fingers between his and tried to explain. "Where I'm from, people aren't allowed to use that sort of physical discipline. Beating a child – beating anyone – can get a person arrested, and their children may even be taken away from them."

"Taken away?" His eyes widened in surprise. "By who?"

Rather than trying to explain all the twists and turns of social work in the twenty-first century, I kept it simple. "The government." I squeezed his hand as my gaze drifted to the cut on his neck. "It's to keep people safe."

"You come from a truly strange time." Gracen slid his arms around my waist and pulled me onto his lap. "Since we are not there, it is my job to keep you safe."

"We'll keep each other safe," I corrected softly. I may have been a woman out of time, but I would do whatever I could to keep the man I loved from harm.

I turned in his embrace, mentally cursing my skirts as I put my knees on either side of his lap. Gracen had taken me to a store yesterday to buy a dress that was more appropriate for someone of my new social standing. Clearly, it hadn't done anything to impress Roston, but Gracen had wanted it, so I'd agreed.

He leaned into my touch as I ran my fingers through his raven-black waves, his eyes closing for a moment. When he opened them again, they were serious. "You are my home, Honor. Far more than these walls ever were. I do not regret for a moment loving you."

The tip of his finger traced my lips, and my nipples hardened under my layers of clothing. He ran his hand through my hair until he cupped the back of my head. My hair was longer now than it had been when I joined the army, but it was still short by these contemporary standards. Still, Gracen seemed to like it, and that was all that mattered to me.

Chestnut was the color my mother had always used to describe my hair. That, as well as my almost silver-colored eyes, had gotten me my fair share of male attention growing up, but only Bruce Pacer had had the nerve to ask me out. I pushed thoughts of my former fiancé aside. The only man I wanted was right in front of me. Bruce wouldn't be born for more than two hundred years, and I was fairly certain I'd fallen out of love with him even before I came here.

I slid my hands over Gracen's firm chest, then leaned back so I could reach beneath my skirts. He sucked in a breath as my fingers skimmed over the front of his pants.

"Honor..." He breathed out my name.

I leaned forward and brushed my lips across his. "Let me show you my gratitude for your protection." I mimicked his way of speaking, earning a smile.

I made short work of the fastenings, then smiled as I wrapped my hand around his thick shaft. Until we'd arrived here, we'd spent the majority of our time since our wedding in bed. At one point, Gracen had expressed his surprise at how much I not only enjoyed sex but initiated it. I'd responded by taking his cock in my mouth and making him shout my name. I'd become intimately familiar with every part of his body, but it hadn't been enough. As I stroked him to a full erection, I wondered if I'd ever have enough of him. It wasn't only having gone so long without sex while I'd been deployed overseas either.

It was him. I wanted him in a way I'd never wanted Bruce.

I locked my eyes with Gracen's emerald ones as I moved over him, the tip of him grazing against my damp curls. His fingers flexed against my waist, but he made no move to take control. I let out a small moan as I slid down on him, taking him one delicious inch at a time. While I loved everything about sex with Gracen, it was this part I enjoyed the most. Not because it physically felt any better than anything else we did, but because, to me, that initial penetration was my reminder that I wasn't alone here, that I'd made my choice for a reason. Feeling him filling me, my body molding around his, I felt complete in a way I'd only ever felt with him. It wasn't like I hadn't been a full person on my own, but rather that there was a part of me I never realized was missing until I found him.

As I settled on his lap, I wrapped my arms around his neck, ran my fingers through his hair. He was the sort of beautiful perfection that artists dreamed of capturing, and he was mine. It wasn't the gold band on my finger that marked us as belonging to each other. No, it was something deeper, more visceral, than that. Something that human language was woefully inadequate to describe.

I rocked back and forth on him, enjoying the little ripples of pleasure that went through me as the base of his cock rubbed against my clit in just the right way. His hands slid down to my ass, gripping it through the layers of fabric that separated almost all but the place where we were joined.

We didn't speak, didn't even kiss. The only sound in the room was the rustle of my skirts as I moved, gradually increasing the pace until the muscles in my legs began to ache. In those moments, nothing else mattered, only that we'd found each other. The birth of a nation. The coming violence. Fiancés and families and loyalties. It meant so little compared to the laws of time and space that had bent, all so that we could be together.

His muscles tensed under my hands, hips jerking as he fought to last. I'd learned in the short time we'd been together that his own pleasure always came second. He not only enjoyed seeing me come apart, he needed it on a level I didn't think he even understood. I belonged to him, heart, body, and soul, and he would do everything in his power to provide for me, whether it be protection or pleasure or anything else that fell in between.

I knew now that I hadn't truly understood the extent of that promise until he'd put himself between his father and me. It wasn't as much the level of physical protection he'd offered, but the choice. He hadn't known me long, and the story of where I was from, when I'd lived, was almost too incredible to imagine, but he'd chosen me over his blood, over the family loyalties that he'd accepted for years.

"Let me take care of you," I whispered as I leaned in for a kiss. I nipped at his bottom lip, soothing the sting with my tongue. "Let me thank you."

I flexed around him, and his body stilled, stiffening as he came with a groan. He fisted his hand in my hair, taking my mouth in a rough, demanding kiss, letting it say all of the things that neither one of us had the words to say. As his tongue twisted with mine, he crushed me against him, the motion putting the right amount of pressure exactly where I needed it, and my climax washed over me.

Even as pleasure flooded my body, it was the sound of his voice saying my name, the feel of him holding me, that mattered the most. I still didn't know how I'd come to be here, but I did know why. It was him. Everything in my life had been leading me to this place, this time, so we could be together.

"I love you." His eyes met mine. "No matter what happens with my father or the war or anything else we might have to face, I will always love you."

"And I'll always love you," I promised.

But even as we stretched out on the bed together, I couldn't help but wonder if what had brought me into Gracen's life would honor the vows we'd made.

Chapter 3

The noise outside successfully pulled me out of a rare deep sleep. It was a kind of braying, an odd, annoying sort of sound, the kind of tactic Wilson would've used to wake me up on an off day when I finally had the chance to sleep in. I sighed as I forced my tired eyes open, and the sight of an unfamiliar ceiling pushed me the rest of the way to full wakefulness. I had a few seconds of sheer panic before I remembered where and when I was, and as I regained context, the sound registered.

It was a horse. And the sound wasn't coming from the direction of the stables, which meant someone had arrived onto the estate. Roston had left yesterday before Gracen and I had woken up, which meant we'd had a relatively quiet and peaceful day despite dirty looks sent my way from the majority of the staff. Any goodwill I'd earned while working in the house was gone now that I'd dared to try to "rise above my station." A not-so-quiet night had followed when we'd retired to our room earlier than usual. The space between my legs gave a pleasant throb at the memory. Gracen had been surprised when I asked him to go harder, faster, but he'd complied, and I'd bitten his shoulder when I climaxed to keep myself from screaming.

I rolled over, but I had already felt Gracen's absence. I pushed the bed sheets aside and groggily climbed out of bed, rubbing my eyes as I looked out the window. My heart gave a weird thud as I saw a familiar figure climbing out of a carriage. Sandy hair, a curvy figure.

Shit.

Clara Stiles. Gracen's former fiancée.

I threw on a dress without worrying about all the strange extra things that went under it. I supposed, technically, it made me indecent, but considering most of the staff considered me little more than a whore, I didn't think it mattered much. I ran my fingers through my hair as I practically ran down the hallway. I didn't care if I looked disheveled. Hell, if it made Clara think about what Gracen and I had been doing all night, all the better.

I scowled, hating how jealous and petty I felt.

"Gracen!" Clara's shrill voice broke the silence that had fallen over the house the moment she stepped inside. I caught a glimpse of a pleased-looking Titus closing the door behind her, and then I lost sight of both of them as I started down the stairs.

By the time I reached the end of the staircase, Titus had disappeared, and I caught a glimpse of Clara's skirts as she swished down the hallway. I followed, fairly certain I knew where she was headed. Gracen liked to retreat to the library when he was looking for some solitude, and it would've been the first place I would've gone to find him.

Before I reached the door, I heard Clara speak.

"Gracen, darling." Her voice dripped something that was both sad and saccharine-sweet at the same time. "What happened?"

I paused just outside the doorway, curious to hear how the conversation would go. I had all the faith in the world in Gracen's love for me. Standing up to his father had been more than enough proof. But I couldn't deny that I wondered how he'd explain things to the woman he'd intended to marry.

"Good morning, Clara." His voice was quiet but surprisingly even. "I assume my father spoke to you before he left yesterday."

"It isn't true. You wouldn't do that to me, to us." A beat of silence, then her voice hardened. "Tell me you didn't marry that...that *servant*. You couldn't possibly break my heart, betray me, for someone who scrubs your floors."

"I did marry her." Gracen paused and then added, "I'm sorry, Clara. I didn't intend to hurt you, but I love her."

Silence again.

"You don't love me anymore?" Her voice broke, and I actually started to feel sorry for her.

She hadn't done anything to deserve any of this. If some mysterious power hadn't pulled me through time, she would've been planning her wedding right now. I didn't truly know how Gracen's life had unfolded in the original timeline, but my gut said that he would've married her. With her and his father pressuring him, he would've joined the British army. My arrival had changed everything.

"No, Clara." His voice was gentle. "I'm sorry, but I don't love you. I never did."

I could feel the tension from where I stood. Clara was barely twenty, which wasn't much younger than me, and in a time where people got married young, she was getting on in years. Still, that didn't mean she was mature. Despite the fact that most people would agree that the time I was from was, in many ways, easier than this one, I had no doubt that Clara lived a much easier life than I had. She'd been pampered, had servants, never had to worry or want for anything. She'd never done a day of hard physical labor. Never been afraid for her life, for the lives of her friends. Gracen's rejection was probably the first time she'd ever been rejected. It must have felt like a slap in the face.

"How could you, Gracen?" It came out as a whisper the first time. "How?!" Her voice rose to a piercing octave.

"Clara," he said, his voice suddenly stern. "That's enough."

Silence for a moment, and then the sugar-coated voice was back. "Gracen, I'm so sorry, I don't know what came over me."

Something in her tone made me uneasy, a sort of suggestive, high-pitched manipulation that said she was a hell of a lot smarter than most people gave her credit for. And that she knew how to use it to get what she wanted.

She continued, "I love you, Gracen, and I know you love me. We can get through this. It doesn't have to be the end."

"Okay, I think I've heard enough," I murmured as I stepped into the room.

Gracen looked embarrassed, though I could've told him that he had nothing to be embarrassed about. He'd been polite, but not overly so. I knew he wouldn't have given into anything she wanted.

"Gracen, dear, would you mind letting Clara and I have some time, just us girls?" I didn't take my eyes off Clara, not even when I felt Gracen's eyes on me.

For a moment, I thought he'd insist on staying, but he started for the door. His hand caught mine as he passed, and he gave it a quick squeeze before leaving me to deal with Clara myself.

"How did you do it?" Clara asked as soon as Gracen disappeared. "Seduce him into your bed? Tell him that you were carrying his child?" Her sapphire eyes were suddenly glowing with fury.

"I didn't seduce him." I kept my voice calm even though I was seething inside. I was being accused by the same woman who'd been trying to steal my husband only a few minutes ago.

Clara's expression twisted into something ugly. "But you took him into your bed. Let him…have his way with you."

I wanted to tell her that if she couldn't say it, she wasn't ready to do it, but that saying was still a couple centuries away from being invented. I also wanted to tell her that it was none of her fucking business how Gracen and my relationship had come to be. But this wasn't my time, and I couldn't treat her like a woman who'd been raised in modern-day America.

"He's my husband, Clara."

She took a step toward me, and I could feel the anger and jealousy radiating off her. "He was supposed to be mine."

I didn't deny it, couldn't. Not when I did feel a little guilty over knowing that I altered the course of her life. "I know."

"But you stole him from me."

I shook my head this time. I'd always hated that phrase. It implied that the person who'd been *stolen* hadn't been involved in the decision-making. "It was his choice, Clara. *I* was his choice. And it's done. We're married."

"I–"

My patience snapped. "Deal with it, Clara."

I barely saw her hand flash out, but then there was the sharp sting of a slap against my cheek. I felt a brighter, hotter pain that I was pretty sure came from one of her nails cutting me. I stared at her, unable to believe what she'd just done, this spoiled little rich girl in her flouncy dress and hair ribbons.

"You pathetic, cheap whore!" She practically spit the words in my face. "I will not let you ruin the plans we had set. This is not over. *We* are not over. When he's tired of rutting with the trash, he will beg me to take him back."

I was back in control again, but that didn't mean I was going to take her shit. "I wouldn't hold my breath if I were you."

This time, when she tried to slap me, I was ready. I caught her wrist before she made contact. Her eyes widened, and for a moment, I saw fear in her eyes, fear that she'd underestimated me. Arrogance quickly replaced it.

"Unhand me."

She spoke like someone used to being obeyed, but I wasn't a servant anymore. I tightened my grip until she winced. I didn't want to cause any real damage, but she needed to know that she couldn't come after me like that again.

"I'll only say this once, so you might want to listen carefully." I stared down at her, using every one of the four inches I had on her. "It doesn't matter who Gracen once was to you, or how you believe he and I came to be together. We fell in love, and we got married. I understand that you're upset, so I'll give you a pass on that pathetic slap." My eyes narrowed. "But it's the only pass you'll ever get from me. If you ever try to hit me again or try to come between my husband and me, there will be *serious* consequences."

I held her wrist a moment longer, then let it go. I raised an eyebrow, inviting her to leave. When she still didn't move, I jerked my chin toward the door. She opened her mouth, and I promised myself that if she said one more ignorant thing, I'd slap her, just to make a point.

A part of me almost hoped whatever was buzzing around in that brain of hers came flying out of her mouth for that very reason. I didn't consider myself a violent person by nature, more like someone who had the ability to use violence if necessary.

She just made me want it to be necessary.

After a few long seconds, she closed her mouth and stormed out of the room. I watched her go, gave myself a minute to calm down, and then went looking for my husband.

Gracen was uncharacteristically quiet the rest of the day. I told him what happened between Clara and me, at least enough to explain the red mark and deep scratch on my cheek. He didn't ask any questions, or even offer any sort of commentary, his expression distant. His silence, more than anything, told me that Clara's words had hit him hard. Honor and dignity were something duels were fought over in this time, and the fact that he'd married me without even breaking off his engagement clearly made him feel like he'd violated that honor.

I told myself that he could still love me even though he wasn't happy with the way he'd handled things, but as the day wore on, the more his silence bothered me. As we both readied for bed that night, a part of me hoped that once we were laying down together, he'd properly talk to me. Hold me. That he'd answer the question I had circling in my mind most of the day.

A question that might have a different answer now than it had before.

He stretched out first but didn't look at me as I blew out the candle and climbed into bed next to him. I wanted him to reassure me. More than that, I needed it. I had to know, for my own peace of mind. I was normally a secure person, but this wasn't exactly a normal situation.

"Gracen?"

"Yes?"

I reached over to run my hand along his shoulder. After a few strokes, my fingers found their way beneath his nightshirt, traced a pattern on his back before moving along his hip. I rested my hand there as I gathered my courage.

"Do you regret it?" I finally made myself ask the question. "Being with me? Marrying me?"

There was a brief silence.

"Why are you asking me that now?" he asked. "I told you how I feel."

"But you've seen more consequences now. If you'd left me where you found me that day, your father wouldn't be angry at you." I paused and then added, "And you wouldn't have broken your word to Clara."

He didn't say anything for a minute, and I told myself it was a good thing that he was fully considering the question and not just blurting out something he didn't mean.

"If I had left you, you probably would have been picked up by the British army. And even being a woman might not have been enough to save you from being called a spy."

That was true, but I hadn't asked him about that. I wanted to know about him, and the fact that he was skirting the question made me think that I probably didn't want to know the answer. I rolled onto my back, tears pricking my eyes.

I should have known that everything he said before had been in the heat of the moment. Emotional. He hadn't really had time to fully process everything that'd happened between us and what it meant. What it was costing him.

I'd lied to him. Made him back out of his promise to a woman from a good family. Made his father angry to the point of striking him.

Even if he hadn't left me on that field, he should've just let me leave after we slept together that first time. He might've thought marrying me was the honorable thing to do, but I wouldn't have held our one-night stand against him. He could've even made himself feel justified letting me go after I told him the truth about where I was from. Either that I was crazy, or that he needed to let me return to my own time. He should have let me walk away any one of a dozen times.

I felt the mattress move beneath me as he rolled over. His arm slid around my waist, and he pulled me back against him, the heat of his body chasing away a chill that had little to do with the night air.

"I don't love her, Honor. I love you. If I had left you behind, I might have married her. My father would have been happy with me, but I would have been miserable." He kissed the back of my neck, and I felt him start to harden against my ass. "And I know that, deep in my heart, I would have lost the only chance I had at loving someone again."

A half sob, half laugh escaped my lips as I rolled over to face him. I pulled his head down for a kiss, digging my hands into his hair as I slid my tongue between his lips. He moaned into my mouth, hips pushing against me. I hooked my leg over his hip, my nightgown – shift – slipping up my thigh, his hand following until he grabbed my ass.

When I finally broke the kiss, I rested my forehead against his but didn't move my body away. His hard length throbbed against me, our skin separated only by the thinnest cotton. All I needed to do was shift a bit to move our nightshirts, and he could be inside me.

A lack of undergarments during this time period had its advantages.

"You came back in time for me, Honor. Nothing I do can ever deserve what you gave up to be with me."

"I didn't really have a choice," I pointed out.

He laughed as he brushed his lips across mine. "Would you have chosen differently?"

I didn't even have to think about it. Not with his arms around me. "Not a chance."

He kissed the top of my head. "Good."

Chapter 4

Gracen looked pensive as he dressed the following morning, and it unnerved me.

"What's wrong?" I asked as I pulled on a plain cotton dress over my shift. I'd done the whole stays and uncomfortable shit the first day we came back. After that, I made sure Gracen knew that me wearing all of it would be a rare occurrence. I needed to be able to move around. And breathe. Breathing was good.

"My father is supposed to return today," he said. "Titus mentioned it to me yesterday evening."

"And?" I prompted, even though I had a feeling I wouldn't like what he had to say.

"We need to talk to him about the future."

I sighed and shook my head. "No, Gracen. We can't do that."

He shot me a confused look. "What do you mean, we can't? I thought we needed to convince him to support the colonists."

"He won't believe us." I stood and crossed the room to stand next to him. "Not when he's so angry right now. He'll think it's all my influence."

I didn't add that if Gracen slipped and said why I believed what I did, that Roston might try to accuse me of witchcraft. I couldn't remember just how that sort of thing would go at this particular point in history, but I doubted it'd be anything good.

Gracen sighed. "That is what my father would think."

I brushed back some hair from his face. "Besides, with the way he's treated you, why do you even want to try to convince him of what's to come?"

His hand went to the back of his neck, eyes sliding away from me. "I suppose I don't like being thought of as a traitor."

I put my hand on his cheek until he looked at me. "You're not a traitor."

"Not enlisting with the British makes my father think that I am. I want him to understand my reasons for not enlisting. Can you understand that?"

I shook my head even as I wrapped my arms around his waist. "I'm sorry, but I don't."

He was quiet for a moment before saying, "You said that you love your father and that he's the best man you know. You wouldn't wish to shatter his good opinion of you, would you? You wouldn't want to remain at odds with him forever." His voice softened. "He's all the family I have. *We* have."

He was right, I realized suddenly. I couldn't simply tell him that my family would accept us, and him. My family wasn't here. Hell, I was pretty sure that most of my ancestors at this time weren't even in this country.

I looked up and saw the sadness in his eyes. In that moment, I knew that I would do whatever I could to erase it. It didn't matter that I thought we could make it on our own, or that Roston would never believe – or probably even care – what we told him. It wasn't about me. It was about Gracen and the importance of family.

"I'm with you, whatever you decide." I tightened my grip on his waist.

I meant it, but I hoped we weren't making a huge mistake.

I tried to be as quiet as possible as I slowly opened the front door, wincing when the hinges creaked. I was hoping I could slip upstairs without running into my dad or my brother. Ennis would pepper me with questions that were simply annoying, and Dad, well, he'd have quite a bit more to say. And he'd give me that look. I didn't want that look.

Slipping off my shoes, I padded toward the stairs in stocking feet, clenching the collection of key chains hanging on the zipper of my backpack in one fist to keep them from jangling. Even the best sneaking, however, wasn't a match for a man with ex-army hearing.

"Honor, come here please."

Shit.

I froze. My father's voice came from his study, and I knew it was no use pretending I hadn't heard him. I'd been caught. I released my key chains, dropped the backpack noisily on the hardwood floor, and then made my way to the doorway of the study.

His laptop was open in front of him, but he looked up when I appeared at the threshold. "Where were you tonight?"

"I told you," I said, tugging the sleeves of my sweatshirt down on my arms so that they almost covered my hands completely. I fidgeted when I was nervous. "I was with Bruce. We went out to dinner, then to a movie."

Dad raised his eyebrows, skepticism clearly written on his face. "It's almost one in the morning."

"The movie started at ten-thirty and lasted two hours. I came straight home afterward. Mom knew how late I'd be."

I almost grimaced at bringing my mom into it, but I really had told her my plans. I reminded myself that I hadn't done anything wrong. Bruce and I hadn't slept together. Hell, we'd barely kissed. True, Bruce had tried to get a little more hands-on, but he hadn't argued when I shut him down. Though it was probably still more than my parents would be happy with, we hadn't done anything wrong. I knew that we hadn't gone too far, even if Dad believed otherwise.

"Can I go to bed?" I knew better than to just say I was going.

"I don't like this, Honor."

Of course he didn't.

I could have tried to explain, but I didn't. Dad was never going to approve of Bruce, and that was a fact. I needed to stop trying to defend my relationship. Nothing was going to change. Not with Bruce and certainly not with my dad. I respected my father's opinion, but my mind was made up, and nothing was going to change it.

The memory had come through clearer than it ever had before, and it stayed with me as our dinner with Roston approached. I knew he'd gotten back at some point today, but between the two of us working to avoid each other, I hadn't seen him yet. While I was glad of that, it did little to ease my anxiety.

"I don't know what to say to him, not after what happened." I smoothed down the skirt of my new dress. It'd been a surprise from Gracen, but I couldn't help thinking that he'd chosen it to make me look more like the proper wife I was supposed to be. However, even the rich mahogany color and the fine material supplied little confidence when I thought about sitting in the same room with Gracen's father, pretending to be civil when all I really wanted to do was slap my father-in-law senseless.

I didn't even want to think about how we could ever convince Roston to change sides in a war that hadn't even been officially declared. A war that no one would believe a bunch of ragged colonists would win, not until it was almost over.

"I need to try to make things right." Gracen glanced over at me, a slight smile forming on his lips. "Also, it will give us an opportunity to show him what an intelligent, amazing daughter-in-law he has."

I knew Gracen meant to be encouraging, but it only made me more uneasy. I knew Gracen loved me, but I was no Clara. I was an army medic, not a socialite. I could triage and fire weapons no one in this century could imagine. But I couldn't smile and flirt to charm a room. I didn't know how to run a household. I'd never be what Roston Lightwood wanted for his son.

"Just follow my lead." Gracen kissed my forehead, then took my hand.

I focused on slowing my breathing and trying to calm my pulse as we made our way to the dining room, but I was still on edge when we arrived. Roston was already seated, a newspaper on the table in front of him. He didn't stand when we entered. In fact, he didn't even look up.

"Good evening, Father."

Gracen managed a much more cordial tone than I could've in his position. His expression stayed carefully blank as his father raised his head. Roston's cold gaze moved from Gracen to me, and I endured his scrutiny without looking away until Gracen pulled out my chair, giving me an excuse to break eye contact. Sitting in these damn dresses was a real pain in the ass.

"How was your trip?" Gracen asked once we were all seated.

Roston's smile was anything but kind. "I don't see why it matters to you, seeing what scant regard you have for the Lightwood name."

My hands curled into fists, but I did as Gracen had instructed and let him take the lead. His father, his place.

"Actually, Father, that is an issue I wanted to address this evening."

"Oh, is it?" Roston raised his eyebrows, his expression as mocking as his tone. "Pray tell, what could you have to say that would undo the irrevocable havoc you've brought upon our good name with your impulsive decision?"

"I don't intend to undo anything," Gracen answered easily. "I know that breaking off my engagement to Clara was handled indelicately and that you don't approve of the choice I made regarding not taking a commission, but I have something that may...help. I only ask that you hear me out."

"Hear you out," Roston scoffed. He didn't even look at the servant who set his dinner in front of him.

"Yes. First, I would like to apologize for what happened with Clara."

My stomach clenched, and I set my fork down. He hadn't told me he planned to talk about her. I would've preferred not to give Roston more of an excuse to discuss all the ways Clara was a better match than I was.

Roston made a scornful noise. "Is that so?"

"Yes. Not for marrying Honor, but for how I went about ending the engagement. It was a business deal, not a matter of love, but I should have faced it head-on."

My father would have praised Gracen for being man enough to admit that he'd handled something wrong, but Roston simply looked bored with the whole thing. It didn't stop Gracen from continuing though.

"Second, the army."

The expression on Gracen's face told me that he was trying to choose his words carefully. I understood the difficulty. When I tried to warn Gracen without telling him who I was or when I was from, I'd simply blurted out the truth about the British losing. I had a feeling that wouldn't work very well with someone like Roston. Hell, it hadn't really worked with Gracen.

"A decision to join the British forces would have destroyed everything. Even if I survived the war, as a commissioned officer, I could be tried as a traitor. If I managed to avoid that, we would most likely have to return to England as we'd never have peace here."

The atmosphere in the room thickened as Roston leaned forward. "And why, Son, do you think that would be the only possible outcome?"

"The British lose the war."

Shit.

The second the words left Gracen's mouth, I knew Roston wouldn't believe him. Color crept up the elder Lightwood's cheeks, and his mouth twisted like he'd tasted something sour.

"This isn't some unorganized group of rebels trying to get attention," Gracen softened his tone, but still persisted. "They believe what they're fighting for, and you know as well as I do that the Crown will not give them what they want."

"The Crown will crush this rebellion," Roston said. "And the soldiers who fought for the King will be recognized for their loyalty."

He sounded so sure of himself, and I knew that was one of the biggest mistakes the British had made. Not that they'd been without reason. They'd crushed every native population they'd fought against so far. The Scottish rebellions had always been quashed, and the Brits had so thoroughly destroyed them only thirty years or so ago that most Scots would fight for the British in this war to avoid being on the losing side again.

The American Revolution was the first time a group of rebels had managed to overthrow tyranny in modern history – or at least as far as I remembered from my history classes – and it would be this rebellion that would give other countries the courage to do the same. France, most notably as their revolution wasn't too far off.

"No, Father, they won't."

Gracen reached over and took my hand, bringing me back from the future to the past...or rather the present. I tried to give him an encouraging smile.

"The colonists will not give up," he continued. "They are fighting for their freedom, and it is not a war the Crown will win."

"That's preposterous. Absurd!" Roston tossed his napkin onto his half-eaten dinner. "The British army is the greatest army in the world. No rabble with pitchforks and sticks will stand against them."

"I'm sorry, Sir," I said with a small voice. Then clearing my throat, I added, "but they aren't without a leader. Washington has their allegiance and their respect."

Roston made a sound of contempt. "Washington is a fool, and if he hangs as a traitor, it will be too good for him." He pointed his finger at Gracen. "I don't care where you have heard this nonsense, but it stops. Now," he said, glancing at me briefly before looking back at Gracen. "You will enlist in the British army, and you will set aside this...*girl* so I may attempt to fix the mess you have made."

"No." Gracen shook his head, his jaw set. "I will not fight for a cause I do not believe in, and I will not set Honor aside. She is my wife, and I made a vow before God and man. It is done." He paused for a moment, and then added, "I love her the way you loved my mother. Would you have given her up?"

Roston pushed back from the table hard enough that I thought the chair would tip over. The expression on his face was nothing short of pure fury.

"Don't speak to me about your mother." His voice shook angrily. "She would be ashamed of you, of the person you've become." He glared at me and then turned his anger back toward his son. "I am only grateful that she died before she could see you make a mockery of everything we worked so hard to build."

He stormed out, nearly knocking over one of the servants as he left. Gracen and I watched in silence, neither of us speaking even as servants scurried around to pick up the things that'd been knocked over before anything was ruined. Only after the last of the dishes had been cleared away did I dare to speak.

"That could have gone better."

Gracen glanced over at me, his eyes filled with dejection. "I had to try."

I mentally cursed Roston for the pain he caused his son, but I couldn't truly blame him for not believing that the British would lose. It was at its height of power, with colonies all over the world. This was the time period when the sun never set on the British empire...and my history buff of a brother had told me that it hadn't just been a saying.

In the eyes of the current world, Britain was unbeatable.

It was ludicrous to assume a war that hadn't even been declared would be won by a country that didn't yet exist. Gracen was taking a leap of faith believing me, and I wasn't about to show Roston my tattoo in the hopes that it would sway him to believe us. All Gracen and I could do now was hope that Roston would come to see the truth before it was too late.

Chapter 5

"You shoulda listened to me."

I jumped, startled, and quickly turned from the library window to find Dye standing only a few feet away. I'd been so deep in thought I didn't hear her enter. I'd been so wrapped up with learning how to run a household that I'd barely seen her and hadn't talked to her outside of the basic instructions I'd given to the whole staff. Technically, Roston was in charge, but Gracen had told me that it'd be a good idea to show an interest in how things were done. I didn't see it hurting anything so I'd agreed.

"Should have listened to you about what?" I asked the question even though I had a fairly good idea what she meant. She wasn't the type of person who kept her opinion to herself, and she'd had a strong one about my relationship with Gracen from the very start.

"You know what," she responded with a nod at me. "Warmin' Master Gracen's bed has caused you nothin' but trouble."

"That's not what's happening. I'm his wife." I held up my hand to show my ring. "And being married to the man I love seems a small price to pay for a little bit of trouble."

Dye shook her head again, her dark eyes gleaming. "But it ain't just a little bit, an' I think you know it. It ain't gonna be pretty when it ends badly."

I didn't like the shiver her words sent down my spine, but I lifted my chin, refusing to let her sense the doubts coming alive inside me. I was determined not to let them take hold.

"You have no idea what you're talking about. Gracen loves me."

She ran her hand over her short black hair and shook her head. "I'm sure he do, but Master Roston ain't ever gonna forgive you for marryin' his son."

I wanted to argue with her, was even tempted to pull rank for a moment, but I knew she was right. No matter how much I wanted to hope that Roston would accept me and the rift between father and son could be healed, a deeper part of me knew Roston would never forgive me, and that he'd continue to blame me for everything that was wrong between father and son.

Scenes flashed in front of my eyes. My first meeting with Gracen. Our escape from the captivity of the British. Coming here. The first night we spent together. Me telling him the truth. Our wedding.

Each memory was more precious to me than the last. Each one reminding me that, no matter what we had given up, it was worth it because we were together.

"It doesn't matter," I finally said. "Gracen may want to make things right with his father, but he won't give me up to do it."

Dye gave me a hard look. "I ain't never been involved with no man, but I seen how men treat women, and they always choose themselves first. When Master Roston tells his son to go marry that

Stiles girl or lose everything, you can bet Master Gracen won't be thinking 'bout that ring on your finger or any pretty promises he made."

Before I could think of a response, she was gone.

When I'd talked to her before I left, I'd hoped her cryptic speech had meant she had some sort of mystical knowledge about what had happened to me. Now, I was hoping it was simply the way she spoke because I really didn't want to consider that she had any sort of prophetic powers. If she did, then the future I thought my marriage to Gracen had prevented might have only delayed it. He might end up with Clara after all.

And I'd be stuck in the past...alone.

The future was something that soldiers either didn't talk about at all or talked about too much. Some saw it as bad luck to talk about the future when the next day could be their last. Some saw it as a way to laugh in the face of the odds. My friends and I, we only talked about it when the end of a tour approached.

The last conversation we'd had like that came back to me with such clarity that I could almost hear my friends' voices.

"Can't wait till I can just sit back at a desk all day," Wilkins said with a lazy grin. *"Easy street, I'm telling ya."*

"So, your ideal reward for making it through four deployments is getting to shuffle papers all

day and count loads of scrap iron?" Rogers said, his hands never pausing from shuffling the deck of cards he carried with him for moments like this. "That's your dream plan?"

"Hey, don't be an ass," Wilkins retorted. "It's a family business."

Rogers snorted, executing a perfect bridge with the cards. "Your face is a family business."

I rolled my eyes. "You two snipe like an old married couple."

Wilkins flipped me off even as he kept after Rogers. "All right, Rogers. What are you planning that's so great?"

Rogers began flicking cards at a hat he'd set a few feet out. "I plan on finally using the teaching degree I sweated over before I enlisted. I'm gonna make some kids smart, y'all."

I laughed as I rolled onto my side. "Not with that kind of English, you're not."

Rogers paused in his card shuffling to give me the finger, a gesture which I returned.

It was our language of love.

"Alright then, your turn, Honor," Wilkins said. "When your last tour's up, when you finally decide not to re-enlist, what're you going to do?"

"Oh, you know, normal stuff," I responded, with a vague wave of my hand.

"Brilliant, Daviot. A real winner."

"I plan on sleeping a lot," I went on. "Maybe eating something that tastes halfway decent."

"Your plan sucks," Wilkins said.

"It's no suckier than yours."

"Yeah, it is. By far."

My eyes returned to the ceiling above me as the boys continued to banter. In truth, I knew exactly *what I wanted. I wanted to finish getting my medical degree. I wanted to get married. Become a pediatrician and open up my own practice. I wanted to settle down and have a family. I wanted to have time to fuss over the simple things in life. To worry about the normal things like bills and groceries and where to go on vacation rather than IEDs and insurgents.*

I sighed as the memory faded. Before the car wreck that had somehow plunged me into a different century, I'd thought those plans would be hard but attainable. Now, I was just hoping Gracen and I would be able to survive the war and have a simple future.

I pushed my hair back from my face and took a deep breath. I'd lingered in the library too long. Then again, if I was going to be completely honest with myself, I'd been hiding and not lingering. In the four days since Roston had returned, he'd made a point of being a complete ass to me every time we crossed paths. Nothing too overt, but always clear enough that I had no doubt where he stood and exactly what he thought of me.

Today was just starting, but tensions were still as high as the day of the argument.

Or, at least, that's what I thought until someone knocked on the door shortly after the mid-day meal. I was partway up the stairs when I stopped and turned back to see who it was.

Part of me expected it to be Clara on the other side when Titus opened the door, but it wasn't. Instead, it was something worse.

Three uniformed British soldiers stood behind a fourth man in a slightly more pristine uniform. He was definitely an officer, though what rank, I didn't know. My brother Ennis would've. A wave of wistfulness washed over me.

Then I remembered what Gracen and I had done to the British soldiers who'd taken us captive, and my stomach flipped, my hand tightening on the railing.

I told myself that I didn't know why they were here. There were plenty of reasons why they could have come unannounced. Considering Roston's known Loyalist tendencies, they'd probably just come by to say hello.

Right?

"May I help you?" Roston asked as he entered the room.

It was the first time I was actually grateful to see him. I wasn't sure I would've known what to say.

"Roston Lightwood?" The officer gave a tight smile.

"Yes?"

"I am Corporal Quincy Axe. Is there somewhere we can speak privately?"

Roston nodded and motioned for them to follow him to the parlor, and all I could do was watch Gracen trail along behind. I knew he had to go, if only to find out the reason for their visit, but I felt sick as the door closed behind him, as if I was somehow abandoning him to something we should face together.

I hovered on the stairs, unsure where I should wait. I didn't like the idea of going up to our room, as if I had something to hide, but I wasn't sure I could take being anywhere near Titus or the other servants right now either. Finally, I decided on my favorite room. It helped that the library was close enough to the parlor that I could keep an eye on the door without seeming like I was doing just that.

It seemed to take forever, even though I knew, in reality, it'd only been less than fifteen minutes. When the door opened and Gracen came out, I called to him before he'd taken more than a couple steps. He crossed the short space between us in only a few quick strides, his expression unreadable.

I forced myself to keep my voice low. "Gracen, what's going on? Why are they here?"

He came to me, his hands settling on my arms, his touch calming me.

"There's no need to worry. We just–"

A booming voice interrupted Gracen's words. "Ah! So this must be Master Gracen's little wife."

After a moment, Gracen took a single step to the side to let me see the man behind him. He wore the signature red coat and white breeches that I'd only seen on the big or small screen. His cocoa-colored hair was wet with sweat, the waves plastered to his forehead. He was tall and muscular, easily standing out as the biggest amongst his companions. Almost as tall as Gracen, he was actually wider.

"Yes, Corporal Axe, this is my wife, Honor." Gracen's voice was polite as he turned toward the soldier, but I could see how the smile he gave the soldier didn't quite reach his eyes.

The man's dark eyes turned back my way, his gaze slowly slithering over me as if hungry. "It's a pleasure, ma'am. Corporal Quincy Axe, at your service."

"It's kind of you to pay us a visit." He made my skin crawl, but I couldn't be rude, not with what was at stake.

"Your husband hasn't told you yet?" Quincy's thin lips twitched. "We're not visiting. We have business in the area and require room and board." He glanced at Gracen. "Which, I'm sure, as loyal citizens to the Crown, you are happy to accommodate."

Right. Government-mandated housing for soldiers.

I found my nails digging into my palms hard enough to leave marks as I widened my smile. "Certainly. Welcome to our home."

Chapter 6

I was in hell. That was the only logical explanation for the past few days. Hell.

Not only did I have to deal with Roston's hostility, but also with the British soldiers whose favorite past-time seemed to be insulting the colonists and bossing the servants around. Or flirting with them. I'd already been forced to make it clear to the staff that they were not required to return any attentions they didn't reciprocate. I didn't care what Roston or Gracen said. If one of those assholes tried to force themselves on one of the servants, they'd be sorry.

The day after Quincy announced their stay, more soldiers had shown up every couple hours until the house was packed with more than a dozen Redcoats. Once I realized that I could barely move without running into one, I retreated to the library, finding it pleasantly free of…guests.

I'd managed to lose myself in books for several hours over the last two days, and I was currently enjoying a collection of poetry. I'd never been a huge fan, but I had to admit that there was something to be said for the rhythm and the imagery.

A quiet "excuse me, ma'am," startled me into

focus. I shot up from my seat, turning around to find Corporal Axe at the door of the library, smiling as if he'd been standing there for more than a few seconds.

I inwardly recoiled at the idea of him watching me while I wasn't aware of his presence, but I kept my expression pleasant. "Yes, Corporal?"

"I wanted to inform you that all of my soldiers have arrived." His milk chocolate eyes ran the full length of my body. "You know, Mrs. Lightwood, you are quite the exquisite creature. It seems a pity to waste your considerable charms in a place such as this."

My smile froze, and I made myself count to five so I didn't completely snap. "I wouldn't want to live anywhere else," I answered honestly. "I love my husband, and I love this country."

Quincy's eyes turned cold, but I couldn't tell if it was my comment about Gracen or about loving this country that had caused the change. Either way, I wasn't making any friends. I excused myself and headed to the kitchen to oversee our evening meal. I made a point of staying busy, moving in and out of the various rooms so that neither Roston or Quincy had the opportunity to speak to me.

I'd spent years having to prove myself to men who thought I didn't belong, of being in a job where women were still fighting for respect and equality, so I knew what it was like to have people considering me a second-class citizen. I also knew what it was to have to be constantly on-guard because the prevention and prosecution of sexual assaults left a lot to be desired.

But I'd always been safe in my home, always had certain team members who I knew had my back.

Here, there was only Gracen, and I knew he wouldn't be able to understand the prickle of unease I got every time I was near Corporal Axe.

After a dinner of pretending that I didn't want to tell the soldiers exactly what I thought of their beloved king, I told Gracen that I wasn't feeling well and made my way upstairs to our room. I lay awake for a while, listening to the murmurs from downstairs, to the creaking house, but I fell asleep before Gracen joined me in bed.

The next day, I woke up at sunrise to find Gracen wrapped around me, his body heat chasing away the faint chill in the air. I knew he must've been exhausted, so I carefully extricated myself from him and the blankets, leaving him to sleep.

I dressed quickly, grimacing at the feel of unwashed skin. I was more used to not always being clean than most of my American contemporaries, but that didn't mean I liked it. Thinking about it, however, didn't help anything, so I made my way down to the kitchen to see if I could find Dye before breakfast. As awkward as some of our conversations had been, I still felt better talking to her than anyone else.

Before I reached the kitchen, however, I heard...singing.

Curiosity piqued, I walked toward it, finding myself heading in the same direction I'd already been going. The sound grew louder the closer I got to the kitchen. Not wanting to go in unprepared, I hid myself in the shadows and peeked inside.

The scene I saw was unexpected, to say the least. Ten drunk men were slurring something that sounded like an English folk song and waving glasses of what appeared to be some of Roston's best liquor. Several servants stood nearby, expressions barely concealing their disapproval. I felt safe assuming that most of them – if not all – hadn't been to bed yet.

"Sirs, Master Lightwood still be abed. If you could lower your voices." Titus sounded more polite than he ever was to me, but I could hear the anger in his voice.

"Shove it, you bloody bastard," one of the men sneered, raising his glass so that some of the amber liquid sloshed over the side. The other men laughed, and the muscles in Titus's jaw clenched tighter.

I definitely didn't want to deal with a roomful of drunk, singing soldiers, so I backed away from the shadows and made my way back up to my room. If this morning was an indicator of how things were going to go throughout the entire war, then Gracen and I needed to seriously discuss leaving before our loyalties were brought to light. The difference between a revolutionary and a rebel was all in which side a person was on, and in a country still owned by Britain, being a rebel could be a death sentence.

I pushed those thoughts aside as I crawled back into bed next to Gracen, willing my heartbeat to slow down. I would have to deal with everything later, and I knew there was nothing I could do about it then, but right now, I could lay next to my husband and forget about everything else for at least another hour or so.

As I tried to will myself to sleep again, I watched Gracen, tracing his features with my gaze. His straight, aristocratic nose. High cheekbones. Soft lips that might've been just a tad too full to be considered manly. His dark waves covered part of his face, and I wondered if this was how he'd looked when he was younger, without the lines and worry that'd come from being ruled by a harsh hand, from losing a wife and child.

"Is it morning already?" Gracen's voice was thick with sleep as he stirred. His eyes stayed closed, but his arms slid around me, pulling me against him. His morning erection pressed against my hip.

"It is," I said softly, snuggling closer to him. "But we have a bit of time before we're needed."

I tried not to think about the men downstairs or the way Quincy's eyes followed me around the room. Of how I'd have to smile and make nice when all I wanted to do was put them all in their place. I hated it, and a part of me even resented Gracen for bringing me back here when we could've made a fresh start somewhere else. Nowhere was really safe for us at the moment, but there were places we could've attracted a lot less attention.

"Honor, my love, is something wrong?"

Gracen's eyes were open now, and even though I could see he wasn't completely awake yet, he was aware enough to have noticed that I wasn't as relaxed as I had been.

I started to shake my head, to tell him that it was nothing, but he stopped me by putting his hand on my cheek.

"I thought we had no more secrets between us."

I sighed. He was right. I'd already told him the worst of it. If he'd been able to accept that I was from the future, I shouldn't ever need to worry about telling him anything.

"It's Corporal Axe," I said. "He's always staring at me, making comments about how pretty I am."

"You are a beautiful woman." Gracen kissed the tip of my nose. "He would have to be blind not to notice."

"It's not that." I shook my head, struggling to find the right words to explain how I felt. "I don't like being alone with him."

"You worry far too much," Gracen said, running his fingers through my hair. "He is an officer in the British army. He would never conduct himself in a less than dignified manner."

I waited for him to say that he was joking, but the expression on his face said that he truly believed what he was saying. I supposed it shouldn't have been surprising. For a man who was almost thirty years old, who'd experienced so much loss, he was surprisingly naive. A part of that, I supposed, came from believing so completely in the idea of honor that he didn't understand people who pretended. It was why he'd wanted to tell his father as much of the truth as possible. He loathed deception. Even a man who did horrible things had his own sort of honor if he was honest about it.

Growing up in the twentieth and twenty-first centuries as I had, skepticism wasn't merely accepted, it was common. People were cynical of everything. Government. Media. Each other. People who took things at face value were mocked. In a way, even those with the most extreme paranoia had a level of respect that the more trusting didn't.

"Conduct yourself in a manner above reproach, and all will be well." Gracen's eyes closed again, signaling the conversation was over.

The worst part of it was that he hadn't said any of it as a warning or even a request. It was evident he simply believed that was the way it would be. As long as I didn't say or do anything that could be misconstrued as inappropriate, then there wasn't anything to worry about. Without that sort of temptation, Quincy would continue to admire from afar and behave as a polite British officer.

And with that statement, Gracen had given his position on the matter. If the corporal did try something, the blame would be on me.

Chapter 7

The only high school dance I'd attended had been my senior prom. Bruce had invited me, and I'd been so head over heels for him that I'd worked my ass off to buy a fancy fitted black dress that constricted my rib cage and high heeled shoes to match. Most girls would've loved the whole build-up, but I'd just been excited to finally get to show people at school that Bruce and I were official, that he was off-limits to the other girls he'd dated while we were casual.

I'd hated nearly every minute of it. The constricting dress. Having all those eyes on me, watching me, wondering what anyone saw in me. Why the man at my side was with me. Hearing all the whispers behind my back. And Bruce hadn't helped. He'd paraded me around like I was some prize, something to show off. At the time, I told myself that it was sweet he wanted people to see us together. It wasn't until we were older that I realized that was just what he did. He showed off with whatever or whoever happened to be around.

When Roston announced that he was holding a party in recognition of our "honored guests," memories of that stupid prom kept coming back. Except it was so much worse.

First, because this was how most people in the area would learn that Gracen and I were married. And since that meant Roston hadn't thrown a party for us, it would show everyone what we already knew.

Roston didn't approve of the match.

Between him and Clara, I doubted anyone in the upper crust of society would be very friendly. The most I could hope for was civility.

Then there was the bigger picture. How to manage myself in a roomful of Loyalists *and* Redcoats without giving away what I thought or felt. And without raising any questions about where I was from or what I knew.

I had to be very cautious when it came to the sort of subtle, yet confusing details that would've come as second nature to someone like Clara. Like who to talk to, when, or how much time was to be spent with one specific guest or the other. Roston had already warned us, more than once, that some of the guests would be coming with the sole intention of catching anyone who could possibly be a traitor. And it wouldn't take much. A simple "the British lose" could land Gracen and me into some serious trouble.

Then there were the more *personal* issues with two of the guests. Our guest of honor, of course, Corporal Quincy Axe, still watched me every chance he got, and he didn't even try to hide the lust in his eyes. The cherry on top, however, was the fact that Clara was on the invitation list. That was Roston's doing, and that wasn't speculation. He told me so personally, looking pleased with himself the entire time.

I wished I could plead a headache and remain in my room for the entire evening, but I knew that wouldn't fool anyone. So, I gritted my teeth and went about overseeing all of the preparations. Like a good wife. Titus would've let me flounder if one of the soldiers hadn't made a comment about the poor quality of pretty much everything. While the steward still despised me, his concern for the family's reputation meant more, so he offered me his wisdom, caustic as it was.

Now, the night was here and the last thing I had to do before guests began to arrive.

Dress.

My gown was made of a deep royal blue silk that I would've loved if it'd been in a different style. And if I didn't have to wear all of the uncomfortable shit underneath. Aside from being unused to how the clothes constricted my ribcage, the layers in the summer heat was nearly overwhelming. I'd dealt with desert heat before, but not when wearing anything like this.

I was attempting to do something with my hair when Gracen came up behind me, placing his hands on my shoulders and leaning over to plant a kiss on my neck.

"You're beautiful," he whispered.

I didn't feel beautiful. I felt awkward, like I was playing dress-up. I didn't fit here, and these clothes didn't make me feel any more comfortable.

"Is that rosewater?" Gracen murmured as he nuzzled behind my ear. His hands rested on my waist as his teeth scraped my earlobe. After a moment, he raised his head, as if sensing I wasn't responding to his attentions with my usual enthusiasm. He frowned. "Are you all right?"

I chuckled dryly. "Your father is hosting a party for Loyalists, British soldiers, and your former fiancée. *All right* isn't exactly the term I would use to describe how I'm feeling right now."

Gracen straightened, removing his hands from my shoulders. "It's not what I would wish for either, Honor, but we have to make the best of it. In a few days, those soldiers will be gone."

I shook my head. "You don't get it. They may say they're only here for a little bit, but the Brits have their soldiers lodged in colonist homes pretty much non-stop. It's one of the things the Constitution will prevent from happening in American."

He gave me a puzzled look.

I simplified it. "Soldiers can't just barge into a person's house and demand room and board." I yanked the ribbon out of my hair and scowled at it. "But none of that matters if I fuck up tonight and say the wrong thing or if your father decides to tell people what you said to him at dinner or…"

Gracen took me in his arms, and I relaxed into his embrace. I wasn't in this alone. He might not have been from my time, but he was with me on this. I just had to keep reminding myself of that.

"I will be right there with you, my love." He pulled back to look me in the eye. "Do you trust me?"

I wrapped my arms around his neck. There was only one response to that question. "Yes, Gracen, I trust you."

I was able to pick up on Quincy's trivial, domineering chatter before I even set sight on his loathsome face. It didn't help that a highly aristocratic group of Loyalists had immediately demanded my husband's attention the moment we set foot into the ballroom. I tried to stick close to Gracen, but in the span of a few seconds, a member of the group had taken him away from me, and I, unfortunately, found myself face-to-face with Quincy.

He held a glass of wine in a slightly quivering hand, taking his sweet time shamelessly eyeing me from head to toe. Shit. He was utterly insufferably sober, and I knew an intoxicated Quincy would be even worse. While the party hadn't technically started until a half hour ago, Quincy had been availing himself of Roston's finest liquor since mid-morning.

I'd taken a couple glasses myself, but I knew my limit, and I hadn't gotten there yet. I actually had a fairly high tolerance for alcohol. I remembered one time on leave when Wilkins, Rogers, and I ventured into the city, and Wilkins had come up with the brilliant idea to go to a bar to see who could drink the most shots while still managing to be able to say a tongue twister without faltering. Since Rogers wasn't much of a drinker, Wilkins had appointed him the judge of the "contest." Wilkins had only proposed that we try such a thing because he seriously believed that he'd beat me. He'd been very wrong.

I'd still been aware of my surroundings and in relative control of myself when Wilkins began to ramble in the middle of the twister, and Rogers had declared me the winner.

I took a moment to be grateful for my tolerance as Corporal Axe leaned toward me, the stench of alcohol wafting off him enough to make my eyes water.

"May I say, you're a heavenly sight if I ever did see one, Miss Honor." Quincy leered at me in a manner I was sure he thought women liked. "We gentlemen of the battlefield rarely get to behold such visions. It's a hard existence, I tell you, but, it is a worthy one, to serve King and Country."

I kept my mouth shut, didn't even smile, hoping he'd finish with whatever it was he had to say. No such luck came my way.

"It would seem that your husband isn't one to agree with me though," Quincy pressed. "Thinks himself too good for the army, does he?"

I clenched my jaw but stayed quiet. Even if it hadn't been a rhetorical question, I wouldn't have given him an answer because he sure as hell wouldn't like what I had to say. I knew what it took to be an honorable soldier, and Quincy didn't have it.

In total disregard to my obvious...displeasure, he laughed, splashing some of the wine in his glass onto the cuff of his immaculately pressed coat. He took a step toward me, and I shuffled back, trying to keep the distance between us without looking like that was my intention.

"Some would see his actions as little better than treachery." He reached out and put his hand on my shoulder.

I was suddenly grateful for the extra fabric that kept him from touching my skin.

"I see them as cowards." His fingers dug in. "Enjoying the privileges that come with his name but never risking anything to protect or defend. And he still somehow manages to find a beautiful woman such as yourself. How is that?"

It was definitely time to get away. With a tight smile, I shook off his hand and stepped past Quincy, scanning the room for my husband. When I finally did spot him, however, I stopped short. Clara had joined the circle of men who'd been monopolizing Gracen since he set foot in the ballroom, and the only description I had for what she was doing was *working the room.* She was conversing animatedly with all of them, her constant laughter reminding me of the clinking of the crystal wine glasses – high-pitched and sharp. The men, on the other hand, appeared to find it enchanting, at least judging by the rapt attention they were paying her.

I couldn't do that. I could figure out how to organize and issue orders so that things would be done on time and done well. I could tell Gracen about the future: the primary battles in the war, as well as advances that wouldn't come about until both of us were dead.

Which, oddly enough, happened to also be before I was born.

But none of that made me a good hostess. Not the way Clara would have been.

Even as I thought it, Clara turned to Gracen, placing her hand on his arm. I saw the gesture as proprietary but told myself I had to be mistaken. She wouldn't do something so inappropriate in front of all of these people. She said a few words that I couldn't make out and Gracen chuckled. Clara added something, causing the other men to laugh again. And her hand didn't move.

Hell no.

I made my way over to the group, smiling hard enough to make my cheeks hurt.

"It sounds like everyone over here is having a good time," I said once I was close enough to be heard. I caught Gracen looking at me out of the corner of his eye, but I ignored him. My temper bubbled under the surface, and I was getting tired of having to hold back. Girls like this pissed me off in my own time. Here, it was worse because the person I'd been in the past – or was it the future? – wasn't someone I could be now.

"We were speaking of the bravery of our men in arms," Clara said, her eyes holding a clear challenge. "And I was telling the gentlemen how fortunate we are to have some of our men actually *here* in our arms."

The men laughed again, apparently finding her play on words just as delightful this time as it had been the first. I opened my mouth, caught a glimpse of a warning in Gracen's eyes...and ignored it.

"And which of our men has been in your arms, Clara? He would have to be a soldier from a good family, wouldn't he? You'd scarcely be able to accept a man of a station any lower than yourself. Come to think of it, though, your family is held in such high esteem that it must be difficult to find any man suitable enough."

I said it all with a smile and the sweetest tone I could muster, but I knew nobody was fooled. Even if they hadn't known about Honor and my encounter shortly after Gracen and I had returned, nearly everyone in the area knew Clara and Gracen had been engaged first.

Gracen's fingers clamped down on my upper arm. "Excuse us, please."

He practically dragged me away from the group, the smile on his face more fierce than friendly. More than one person stared after us, whether because they'd heard what I said or because of the way Gracen was trying to hurry me from the room, I didn't know, but we were definitely attracting a lot of unwanted attention.

When we finally reached a semi-secluded corner, Gracen spun me to face him. "What were you thinking, Honor? Would you care to explain yourself?"

I lifted my chin in defiance, refusing to let myself feel bad about it. "No, I wouldn't care to. She's a guest here, not the damn Queen of England."

That would've been funny if I hadn't been so pissed.

"Honor, we talked about this," Gracen said, his jaw clenched. "You need to attempt to be socially acceptable with these people. We are literally surrounded by people who could have us arrested with a single word. Your petty jealousies are not worth the risk."

I stared at him as he turned away, heading toward a distinguished-looking man with a pipe. What the hell just happened? Had Gracen seriously scolded me, then left me standing here like he'd given me a fucking time out? He hadn't said a word to Clara when she'd been touching him, but I said something he didn't like and he treated me like a child.

I leaned against the wall in a woefully unladylike fashion, watching my husband as he fell into conversation once again. He conversed effortlessly with everyone he spoke to, his manners perfect, his demeanor relaxed. Dealing with events like this was probably second nature to him. After all, this was what he'd been raised to do.

Except I'd changed all of that, turned it all upside down and inside out. My arrival had interrupted the natural course of things, changed destinies. Clara should have been the host of this party, smiling and talking as she moved around the room on Gracen's arm. No matter how angry I was at her, I knew if she understood the truth of what really happened, she would have every right to hate me even more than she already did.

I sighed and pushed myself off the wall. I'd made a mistake, thinking I could do this. The next moment I saw Gracen free, I'd tell him that I had a headache, then head upstairs, leaving him to make apologies for me. The men wouldn't think twice about it. After all, we women were such delicate creatures.

Before I could put my plan into action, however, the hairs on the back of my neck stood up as I felt someone's eyes on me.

Surprisingly enough, Quincy wasn't holding a drink. If he had been, it would have most likely ended up all over my silk gown because his movements were jerky and unpredictable as he sauntered over to me, not stopping until the skirt of my dress was pressed against his pants. I stiffened, trying to slide away as imperceptibly as possible.

"What are you doing over here all alone?" Quincy asked. His breath and voice were both thick with intoxication. "Did your coward of a husband desert you?"

I turned to face him, hands curling into fists. "He's not a coward." My voice was low with fury.

Quincy rolled his eyes, leaning toward me.

"There is no need to argue. I came here to ensure that the most beautiful woman here had the good fortune of dancing with someone worthy of her."

"I don't dance," I said. I wasn't about to tell him that hell would freeze over before he was "worthy" of me.

Quincy moved toward me, snaking one arm around my waist and yanking me against him. "You wouldn't deny a war hero one little dance, would you, Mrs. Lightwood? Surely not!"

"Let go of me," I hissed. I didn't care who he was. No one manhandled me without my permission.

Quincy chuckled, his foul breath invading my senses. When he made a move to touch my face, I pulled my leg back, preparing to knee him hard in the groin. Before I had the chance, he spun us around so that my back was against the wall. My feet got tangled up in my petticoats, and I cursed the fashion of the day.

"Come now, Miss. There's no need to pretend with me." His free hand moved up to the front of my dress, squeezing.

Or, at least, attempting to do so. One good thing I could say about all of the shit that went under this dress. It made over-the-clothes groping a little more difficult.

"I'm not pretending." I turned my face to the side, partly to escape his breath, but also partly because I didn't want him to see on my face exactly how I felt about him. "I don't like dancing."

"I believe there is another sort of *dancing* you and I could enjoy." He breathed hot air on my throat with every word. "I have yet to find a single woman on this god-forsaken continent who can give me what I want. But I think you could."

"I'm a married woman." I spoke from between gritted teeth. "And I want you to get your hands off me."

"Come now," he rubbed against me, "no need to pretend to be coy."

Then something hot and wet slid up my neck, and I froze.

He'd licked me.

The British bastard had fucking *licked* me.

"Corporal Axe."

Relief rushed through me at the sound of Gracen's voice. My previous anger at him melted away. It wasn't his fault that Clara wouldn't accept that the relationship was over. And it wasn't his fault that his father was being such a stubborn asshole. We were both walking a fine line here, risking a lot. We needed to work together, not apart.

All of that went through my mind in a matter of a couple seconds. Barely long enough for Quincy to shift his gaze to Gracen.

"Your wife is quite the accommodating host, Mr. Lightwood."

"Is she now?" Gracen's voice was tight, and when I looked over at him, his eyes were cold.

"Get off me." I shoved at the soldier's chest. He leered down at me a second longer, letting me feel his erection before he took a step back.

"Now, now, Mistress. You weren't protesting my attentions a moment ago."

Heat flooded my face, all fury, though it could've looked like embarrassment from the outside. "Gracen," I started.

"I believe my father is calling for the final toast," he interrupted. "You'll want to be out there,

Corporal." His voice turned to steel. "No worries. I shall look after my wife."

As Quincy walked away, Gracen's eyes finally turned to mine, and I knew this was far from over.

Chapter 8

After the last guest had been escorted out, and the servants given their final orders for the night, Gracen and I said a terse goodnight to Roston before heading upstairs. We'd avoided looking at each other, touching each other, and judging by the smug expression on Roston's face, the tension between us was palpable.

As we made our way up the stairs, I allowed myself a quick sideways glance. Gracen's shoulders were squared, his body stiff. He was clearly furious, but he wasn't the only one. The events of the night hadn't exactly been pleasant for me either.

I strode into the room first, yanking at my hairpins, unintentionally ripping out a few hairs in the process. I ignored the slight sting as I bent to pull off my shoes, hiding a flinch when Gracen slammed the door behind us. He stormed across the room, but I didn't acknowledge his obvious frustration, instead resuming my work on my shoes. I straightened as he walked up to me. I could see him in my peripheral vision, but chose to continue ignoring him. If he had something to say, he could damn well say it.

"How much further do you intend on damaging my reputation, my family's reputation? I understand that you are from a different time period, but I do not think it is too much for me to ask of my wife a single night of decorum."

I released an unladylike snort of disbelief. "Really, Gracen? You didn't seem to have a problem with flirting as long as you were on the receiving end of it. Or maybe that was just for wealthy socialites who want you in their bed."

His eyes narrowed. "Clara was acting the part of a hostess, which is more than I can say for you. Blatantly throwing yourself at an officer in the royal army. Anyone who cared to look could see how you chased after him."

I stared at him, shocked into silence for several seconds as I tried to process the accusation. "*I* went after him? Are you seriously saying that I *wanted* him to act that way around me?"

Gracen crossed his arms, a deep flush working its way up his neck. "Why else would he put his hands on you? He's a commissioned officer who would have no difficulties finding a woman to return his affections. Why would he need to resort to forcing his attentions on a woman like you?"

The words hit me like a punch to the stomach. A woman like me. After all this, that's what I was to my husband. Pain mixed with anger, reducing my voice to a whisper. "And what sort of woman is that, Gracen? What sort of woman did you marry that the only way a British officer would want to grope her would be if she encouraged him?"

The color in his face drained away, leaving his skin mottled. His expression said that he knew he'd made a mistake, but my temper was building again, and I wasn't going to let him brush this aside.

"For your information, that asshole didn't care when I reminded him that I was married or that I didn't want him touching me. I was trying to be polite for the sake of your precious reputation, so instead of slapping him like he deserved, I tried for some passive resistance. That was my second mistake. My first was thinking you were any different from the rest of the chauvinistic bastards who would rather blame the victim than take responsibility for their fucking actions."

Gracen stared at me, eyes wide. I knew I was on the verge of losing control, but the reality of what happened – what *could* have happened – had finally hit me. I'd spent years in the service, knowing that for every good guy like Wilkins and Rogers, there were others who wouldn't think twice about forcing themselves on me. And that a system of good ol' boys would probably protect them. I was under no illusions that things were better for women here, but I thought that I'd at least have Gracen on my side.

"Axe was right about you," I said, voice shaking. "You are a coward." He flinched, but I kept going. "Biding our time to announce our loyalties is smart, but now I'm thinking that isn't why you wanted us to pretend tonight. You'd rather play the game, smile at those men, flirt with Clara...blame me, than risk saying or doing anything that would make you look bad."

I winced when Gracen wrapped his hand tightly around my arm, his fingertips digging into my skin hard enough to bruise. "You know nothing of what I thought. My reasons." His voice was low with fury. "You have no idea what I've put aside for you. What I've lost and still could lose. None at all."

His words broke my heart, a reminder that just because he hadn't left his family and friends behind didn't mean any of this was easy for him. "You can get it all back," I murmured. "If I...disappeared, no one would think twice about whatever explanation you gave. You could marry Clara. Stay out of the war completely or join the British. Use what I've told you to try to change the future. Forget about me."

Gracen's grip loosened around my arm. He looked at me in disbelief as he shook his head, his anger vanishing. "I could never forget about you."

I brought my hand to his cheek. "Then what happened tonight?"

He ran his hand through his hair. "All week, I've seen him watching you, the corporal. I know what a man like him could offer you. What I said, that phrase, *a woman like you*, it wasn't an insult. You are so far above me, above him, that I told myself the only way he would dare approach someone as beautiful and amazing as you would be if you allowed it."

He reached out and cupped the side of my face, stepped into me and slid one arm around my waist. The pain in his eyes spoke to the truth of what he was saying.

"I was afraid I would lose you. I can bear giving up everything, so long as I have you." He lowered his head, capturing my lips with a kiss, his hand moving to bury itself in my unbound hair.

We were so different, came from such different places, and the longer we were together, the more obvious it became. But none of that mattered because what he said was true. I could give up my time, my family, friends, job, technology – hell, indoor plumbing – as long as he was with me. It was that, I realized, that had triggered my actions when it came to Clara. I'd never been a truly jealous person, but seeing her with Gracen hadn't only given me a flare of envy. Fear had been the motivating factor. Fear that he'd realize he'd made a mistake choosing me, and I'd be stuck in this place and time alone.

"I'm sorry," I murmured, sliding my hands up his chest. "I was scared too."

"Of what?" He looked so puzzled that it eased the knot around my heart.

"That you'd realize you made a mistake. Choosing me."

He took my lower lip between his teeth, worrying at it for a moment before soothing it with his tongue. "You are the best decision I've ever made, my love."

I took his mouth this time, pouring everything I felt into the kiss, letting him feel how much he meant to me. How much I loved him. How he was the only man I wanted. The only one I'd ever want. And I knew that now. If I was taken away from him, sent back to my own time, he would still have my heart.

"Promise me you'll never let Clara Stiles touch you again," I said, biting at his jaw. "I'm the only one allowed to touch you."

"Never. I'd be a fool to want anyone other than you," he said, his hands working on the first of the many layers separating us.

I loved the strength I could feel in his arms, in his hands. There was passion in his touch, so much so that I couldn't exactly call him gentle as he stripped off my dress, but there was no fear in me, no worry that he could hurt me. Even in our most intimate moments, when he allowed himself to lose control, he protected me.

When I was finally down to my shift and him to his nightshirt, we collapsed onto the bed, hands sliding over and under the coarse fabric, his need to touch me matching my own. His kisses were rough, teeth scraping, mouth sucking until I knew my skin would be marked. I didn't care, meeting each bite with one of my own, raking my nails down his back, over his ass. He was mine.

The world began to fade away. Roston, Clara, Quincy, Bruce, everyone. This was what mattered. This was all that mattered.

At some point, the last of our clothing ended up on the floor, baring our bodies in the flickering candlelight. I knew a lot of couples during this time kept their rooms dark when they made love, but I wanted to see him, needed to see him. His long, lean body, defined muscles. The dusting of dark hair across his chest that trailed down to the base of that thick, beautiful shaft.

I cried out as he took a nipple into his mouth, sucking hard, sending a direct bolt of pleasure straight through me. I hooked a leg around his hip, rubbing against his cock. He moved his hand between us, and I braced myself for the overwhelming sensation of fullness that came with him sliding into me. But it was a finger that probed between my lips, that moved over my clit, and then down, before slipping inside.

I gasped out his name, closing my eyes as his mouth and hand drove me toward climax. I shuddered as I came, then cried out when he pushed inside. My still trembling body opened to him, accepted him, welcomed him.

"Perfect," he breathed against my skin. As he rocked against me, he raised himself on his elbows so he could look down at me. "Perfect how we fit together. Two hundred years separated us, and yet we were made for each other."

I reached up, ran my fingers through his hair. "I've never really had much belief in a higher power, in fate or destiny, but you…you make me believe."

He buried his face against my neck, his thrusts coming harder and faster as he chased our release. I meant what I said, that he made me believe in something greater, but there was something more that I hadn't said. That if whatever had brought us together decided to tear us apart, I'd never forgive it. I'd made my choice to give up everything for him, and I'd be damned if I let him go without a fight.

As I came again, I let go and screamed, tightening around him until he cried out my name. I didn't care if anyone heard us. In fact, I hoped everyone heard. Then they'd know that Gracen was mine and only mine. And I was his.

Chapter 9

I rolled over, squinting as the morning sun blazed against my face. The maid must have already entered the room to open the shutters and let in some fresh air. I hadn't heard a thing. The idea of servants wandering around during moments of vulnerability still made me feel weird, but I knew better than to say a word. I already drew enough attention to myself by refusing to let anyone bathe and dress me. Well, for the most part when it came to dressing. The more complicated gowns required a second or third set of hands. That couldn't be helped.

I reached for Gracen, propping myself up on one elbow to kiss his jaw. I moved my mouth slowly up to his, my hand sliding over his firm chest toward my goal. My lips brushed against his, and I stopped when he didn't respond. A knot formed in my throat as I remembered the morning after our first night together. A morning when all of the magic of the evening before had dissipated, and he'd accused me of wanting to use him.

I'd hoped we were past that, but I wouldn't know unless I asked. "Gracen?" I said his name tentatively, hating myself for the timidity.

"What?" he asked, still not looking at me.

"What's wrong?"

I was only slightly reassured when he slipped his arm under me to encircle my shoulders. The relationship between husbands and wives in this time and place was something of a mystery for me. While history said that women had a lower place in society, I knew that history books rarely had the full story, especially when it came to what went on behind closed doors.

"I'm thinking."

I hated my need to ask Gracen again about his devotion to me when he'd demonstrated both verbally and physically that he was mine, but the urge to do just that was strong. I was grateful when he spoke first.

"We need to leave, Honor."

A rush of relief washed through me, but I forced myself to temper my excitement. I needed to be sure that I understood correctly. "You mean leave here?"

"Yes."

I sat up, needing to see his face to know that he was serious. I caught the sheet against my breasts. I didn't care about the nudity, but distractions were a bad idea right now. I wanted his full attention for a completely different reason.

"What about your father? Convincing him to join the cause? Upholding your family name?"

I watched my husband's face as he formed his answer, as he struggled to understand it himself. I traced my finger along his forearm, giving him all the time he needed. He was physically strong, more so than a lot of men of his class, but it was his strength of character I'd come to admire and love. He'd tried to hide it under the guise of familial loyalty, but I saw it as clearly now as I ever had.

"I cannot continue to play the role my father wishes me to play. He has made his choice, and I have made mine. I need to follow through, and I do not believe I can do that here."

I knew that this decision hadn't been easy for Gracen to reach, and my heart broke for the pain I knew he must be experiencing. I gave him a soft kiss before resting my head on his chest. The steady thump of his heart was comforting, soothing. It was home more than any four walls and a roof could ever be.

"Thank you," I said.

"No, thank *you*." He kissed the top of my head. "You've changed everything for me, Honor."

As I rested there, I reminded myself that I had the future on my side. The sacrifices Gracen was making now would be proved right before this was all over. It wouldn't make what we had to do easier, but we weren't doing this on blind faith. I knew that the United States would come to be, and while far from perfect, it would justify all of the pain we'd go through. Well, it wasn't blind faith on my part. For Gracen, he had to place his trust in me, and being willing to leave was definitely showing that trust.

In some ways, it reminded me of how it'd felt in my unit while we were overseas. I'd been there to stitch them up, take care of their wounds, and they'd had my back. Trust had been crucial there, and it was still crucial here and now. Gracen had to trust that I had his back on this one, just as I had to trust that he had mine.

I ran my hand along Gracen's chest, the gesture more absent than seductive. "Where do you want to go?"

Gracen answered quickly enough for me to know that he'd already thought that far ahead. "Go to Washington and offer our services. He'll be able to tell us where we'd be of the most help."

I scrambled to a sitting position so quickly that Gracen's expression registered surprise. That was definitely *not* what I'd been thinking. I'd assumed we'd hide out somewhere, let the war play out the way it had in my past.

"Go to Washington? As in, George Washington?"

"Yes." He seemed puzzled by my reaction.

"Honey, this is history in the making. I don't think we should interfere." The possible ramifications made my blood run cold. "We could accidentally change everything."

He reached out and caught my hand, bringing it to his lips. "How do you know that what we have done so far has not already made changes?"

Shit.

I felt the blood drain from my face.

"So," he continued, "does it not make sense for us to insert ourselves into the action to ensure that your world comes to be?"

I stared at him. "You seem to have given this a lot of thought."

He shrugged. "The choices we make will have far-reaching consequences."

He was right. About all of it. For all I knew, in the original timeline, the soldiers Gracen and I had killed, Gracen himself, could've had a major impact on choices the British army had made. A different scout or member of the infantry could make different choices, lead to new information the Brits hadn't had before. It wasn't only the big players like

Washington and Jefferson who'd determined the course of the war. Every person had played their part, and my presence could have changed any piece of it.

"All right," I said finally. "We'll try to find George Washington."

A sentence I never thought I'd say.

"It will take a couple days to gather the supplies we need and make our travel arrangements. I think it best if we don't announce our intentions."

"Where will we go?" I asked my original question again.

"Another reason to make preparations while we wait. We need to find out where Washington will be. With his importance to founding your country – *our* country – he is the one whose future we must guard the most."

I'd nearly forgotten that there was no White House for him to stay sequestered away like a celebrity. I'd forgotten that, right now, he was an officer and not a very popular one. Looking into the past, we could see the founding fathers as underdogs who rose above expectations to become great, but in their own time, no one could imagine what their lives would become, what the world-wide ramifications of this war would be. How it would turn everything upside-down.

I shook my head, still trying to wrap my mind around it all. Just when I thought I had a grip on it, something new would come along and throw me for a loop. My stomach tightened at the implications.

"What do you think we'll do for Washington? Join the army?" I ran my hand through my tangled hair. "I suppose I could disguise myself as a man again, even though that would make our relationship awkward. But I am a medic, so I could offer my services as a nurse." While female nurses wouldn't officially be recognized until the Civil War, they'd still been present for prior wars, including this one.

"I was thinking more along the lines of offering to act as civilian spies," he interrupted my thoughts. "It might be valuable to have a few inconspicuous figures working alongside those fighting."

Spies. Right. That hadn't ended well for Nathan Hale, though not for another year if I remembered correctly. I was starting to wish I'd have been more eager to read a few of Ennis' history books so I'd have more details to know how to keep us safe. As it was, I'd have to balance what I did know with what would be the best for the country.

Like Hale. I knew he was executed in the fall of 1776, and that he'd been reported to say, "I only regret that I have but one life to lose for my country." There was some debate about whether or not he'd actually said that verbatim, but there was no doubt that reports of how he'd conducted himself had been responsible for sparking quite a bit of the zeal that went into winning the war.

If I tried to save him, would that make things better or worse? Would America win the war faster with another spy on the inside? Or would the lack of his sacrifice mean fewer people would support the cause?

Or from the opposite side of things. Benedict Arnold. I didn't know much about why he'd become a traitor, or even much of the circumstances around what he did. But his name would become synonymous with treachery, so it clearly had some impact. If I tried to report him before he'd started spying, I could prevent it from happening altogether, or make matters worse by warning him to be more careful so that he didn't get caught...which could have turned the tide of the entire war.

I was starting to get a headache.

I pulled my knees up to my chest, my head swimming with all the possibilities. "Are you sure you want to go so far as to personally offer our services to the colonists? Not supporting the British is a long way from offering to turn on your country."

"I'm certain," he said firmly.

I knew that I didn't look convinced because he chuckled softly, running his fingers through my tousled hair.

"I have never completely agreed with how things have progressed in the colonies, nor with England's treatment of the people here, but I have always kept my opinions to myself. Now, because I believe that what you say will happen is the future for this country, I know that I cannot remain silent any longer."

I kissed him, putting everything I felt into it. I'd been worried that he was starting to lose his faith in me, but I knew now that we were truly in this together. Knowing how much rested on my shoulders was daunting to say the least, but I could do it as long as I had him.

I wasn't present when Gracen told his father

that we were leaving on the thirtieth of the month. I wasn't sure what excuse he'd given, and I didn't ask any questions. I knew that Gracen would have done everything in his power to keep from severing ties with his father completely, but I couldn't care less if we were welcomed back into the Lightwood estate. Personally, I was hoping Washington would want us somewhere like Philadelphia or even New York. I knew that the Sons of Liberty had been going head to head with British troops for the past ten years in New York and that battles would be fought there in the coming years, but that made it even more important to have strategic people in place.

I just didn't want to have to come back here.

The majority of the staff were mercifully absent as Gracen and I departed. The only servants assisting us were the two stable hands who made sure that our horses were saddled and ready. Dye hovered in the background, a distracting, somewhat fiendish grin on her face. I tried to ignore it but couldn't help myself. Every time I looked over, she was looking right back. I still wasn't superstitious, but she had me wondering again if she knew something I didn't. Or she was just thinking that Gracen and I getting away from Roston would be good for our marriage.

Knowing I wouldn't get an answer – at least not anytime soon – I forced myself to give her an acknowledging nod and then set my mind on the journey ahead.

We set out on horseback with two horses that Gracen had purchased himself. He'd been careful to cultivate his own money over the years, not wanting his father to be able to hold his inheritance ransom. Considering that Roston probably would have done just that in regards to Gracen's recent decisions, I was grateful my husband had such foresight. I might not have been used to riding, but it was definitely preferable to walking.

We traveled late into the night, wanting to put as much distance between us and the estate as possible. By the time we finally stopped at an inn, my entire body ached, and I knew I was going to be sore in the morning. Gracen had managed to learn the general direction of the camp where Washington was located. Since he'd only taken command of the Continental Army earlier this month, I was hoping he'd be open to expanding his information network.

After a quick wash down, I fell into bed next to Gracen, who was already snoring and allowed the exhaustion of the day to pull me under.

All I could think about was that I had to get him to the Jeep before he bled to death in front of me. Gunfire filled the air, and I knew that Jacobs wouldn't survive the massive leg wound he'd sustained if I didn't treat him soon. I already knew where I'd put the box containing the medical supplies I needed. That was, if Wilkins hadn't been an irritating scoundrel and rearranged everything. I told him never to move the medical kits without my permission, but sometimes he did shit just to piss me off, regardless of the consequences. That was one of the reasons why I was always having to

bail his ass out of trouble.

I supported Jacobs as best I could, half dragging him toward the truck. He groaned in pain every time I jostled his leg, but it couldn't be helped. When I finally managed to get us both into the relative safety of our transport, I found the kit and got the kid patched up as best I could. He would survive until we made it to the field hospital where I could finish the job.

I'd just given Jacobs a pain killer that I kept stashed aboard when another soldier appeared at the back of the truck. Between the dirt covering his face and the lack of moonlight, I couldn't tell who he was, but that didn't matter. He told me what I needed to know.

"There are way more where that came from, Daviot. Hurry."

I emerged from the back of the truck and followed the soldier around the corner of a half-bombed house to see a dozen men and women lying around what remained of another transport vehicle. The scent of burning flesh invaded my nostrils, and I had to force back the bile that wanted to rise. The continued gunfire was deafening, but I could still hear the scream and cries of pain. The closest body to me I recognized as the other medic, which meant I was the only hope these soldiers had, and the knowledge paralyzed me.

Dimly, I was aware of someone shouting my name, and I knew I had to move or everyone would die, but I couldn't make my legs obey...

I woke up in a cold sweat, struggling to sit upright but constricted by the bed clothes which had become wrapped around my body. Then I felt my husband's touch and heard his voice close to my ear, grounding me as he untangled me.

"Ssshhhh," he comforted, running his hands along my back and shoulders in smooth, soothing motions. I buried my face in his chest as I gulped in deep breaths of air. He ran his fingers through my hair, murmuring words of solace.

"A nightmare?" he asked.

I nodded against him. I hadn't thought or dreamed of my past so vividly in weeks, and half of the shock came from that. The other half, I knew, stemmed from what I knew was to come. I was about to become part of a war that would spark revolution around the world and bring to end one of the greatest empires that had ever existed.

Crippling fear of battle had never before plagued me. But this was beyond the fear of injury or death. This was fear of failing and knowing what it would mean if I messed something up. Gracen's presence, however, reassured me, reminded me that I could do anything with him at my side.

I lay awake long after his breathing became even again, and he fell back to sleep. The beat of my heart slowly returned to a normal rhythm as I spoke reality over and over again in my mind. *Gracen was here. What we were doing was right. Everything was going to be okay. We could do this.*

Like many other things when it came to history, the American camp was far less remarkable than TV had led me to believe. The settlement was a crude one and far from being glamorous. It was late afternoon, the first of August, when we spotted the sentries moments before they called attention to themselves.

As Gracen had suggested, I kept quiet and to the background as he spoke, first to a sentry and then to an officer, before the two of us were led toward a tent near the center of the camp.

"General Washington," the man spoke as he pulled aside the tent flap and stepped inside, "there's a man, Gracen Lightwood, here to see you."

As we followed the soldier inside, a man behind a desk stood and then stepped around with his hand out.

"Hello, Mr. Lightwood," he greeted. As he shook Gracen's hand, he glanced at me, gaze zeroing in on my left hand. "And you must be Mrs. Lightwood."

He looked like the pictures I'd seen in Ennis' textbooks. Tall, especially for this time period. Only an inch shorter than Gracen. He wore the traditional wig that was featured in historical portraits. The main and most salient difference was he was utterly and completely real. As in human. There was a very mortal ruggedness about him. I supposed it was weird because I was so used to seeing actors looking sort of like the historical figure they were portraying, that seeing the real thing was...strange.

"Good morning, sir," Gracen said. He didn't look the least bit nervous. "My wife, Honor, and I have come to offer our support and assistance."

Washington motioned for us to take a seat on the two chairs sitting across from his desk. Everything was on the rickety side, but as a general, he at least got to have furniture.

"Lightwood," Washington said as he took his own seat. "You are the son of Roston Lightwood?"

"I am. You know my father?"

Washington shook his head. "By reputation only." He tilted his head, giving us both a hard look. "He's a Loyalist."

"Yes, he is," Gracen answered. "But his views are not mine. That is why I'm here."

Washington's look was contemplative as he turned his gaze to me. "And you, Mrs. Lightwood? Why have you accompanied your husband? Surely it would be safer for all involved if you remained at home."

Though the statement was made with unmistakable respect, I knew he was simply saying what most men of this time believed. While some women might have been used as nurses, there wouldn't have been many of them.

I wasn't about to let any of that stop me from stating my piece. "I might be a woman, but this is as much my fight as it is my husband's. I would be prepared to work alongside him in whatever capacity you deem fitting."

A few moments of silence passed as Washington regarded us carefully. I could almost see the wheels in his head turning. Unfortunately, I didn't know enough about how he'd strategized to know what he could be thinking.

"Perhaps you're in need of...information?" Gracen suggested. "I have no experience in the army, but my civilian position may provide some useful insight."

Washington stroked his chin. "It's an intriguing concept."

I wasn't sure if that meant he was seriously

considering it, or if he was just playing along, but there was something I knew that might prompt him to make a decision. I just had to figure out the best way to say it.

"Sir," I said, drawing his attention to me. "When King George refuses any agreement the colonies might attempt to make with him, when he officially declares the colonies to be in rebellion – and he will – it will be helpful to have civilians working on your side. Not only as informants but also to pass information along. Civilians rarely get noticed. Especially young *men* of indeterminate birth."

I watched as understanding dawned on the general's face.

"Am I understanding that you are volunteering to impersonate a man in order to gather and pass information?" Washington responded.

I sent Gracen a sideways glance, and he gave me a nod that told me to continue. "It wouldn't be the first time I've played the part of a man, General Washington."

"Though I know that Honor would be more than capable of working under that guise," Gracen put in. "I would wager that the fact that she is female could also be a valuable asset. And a husband and wife who have connections among Boston Loyalists..."

I had to admit, that was better reasoning than some sort of *womanly wiles* shit.

"I will consider your offer," Washington said. He thought again for a few moments and then looked back at me. "What makes you so certain that the king will not negotiate? That he won't listen to reason?"

I made sure I kept eye contact, made my voice even, so there'd be no doubt of my honesty. "By

Thanks..." I cleared my throat to cover my near mistake. Thanksgiving wouldn't be a holiday for nearly a hundred years. "By the end of November, King George will announce to Parliament that the colonies need to be dealt with. This won't be a short skirmish that will be settled quickly."

He looked at me oddly, then after another moment asked, "And why are you so sure of this, Mrs. Lightwood?"

Gracen's hand grasped mine, squeezing it to give me a warning I didn't need. If I claimed to be from the future, not only would we lose all credibility, I'd be lucky not to be accused of being mad...or a witch. Neither of those things had a good outcome.

After a moment, Washington waved his hand dismissively. "Thank you for your offer and your information. I will speak with my men and contact you if we believe you can be useful."

Gracen and Washington shook hands, and I took a minute to appreciate it.

My husband was shaking the hand of America's first president. I'd talked to George Washington. I could end up working for George Washington...as a spy for the Continental Army.

Ennis would never believe it.

Then I remembered that I'd never get the chance to tell my brother about any of this.

Chapter 10

We were back at the Lightwood estate two days later, which was two days too soon in my opinion. Roston's greeting at our arrival was far from warm, but it wasn't extremely hostile, so I figured that it was a good halfway point to settle in at, and probably the best scenario we could realistically hope for.

We'd made decent time back despite my reticence to return, so we had time to wash up before dinner. We didn't talk, but we didn't need to. We'd talked over things the whole way back, going over what I knew the next couple months held – not much that I could remember until George's announcement – as well as discussing what we would do if Washington did call for our service. Better to make plans and not need them than to be caught off guard.

Especially when being caught off guard meant being executed for treason.

When I finally felt clean again – or at least as clean as I could possibly feel without indoor plumbing – I slipped into one of my "proper" dinner dresses, then sat at the dressing table to brush out my damp hair. Gracen came up behind me, leaning close to kiss my neck. When he slid his hand down my shoulder to cover my breast, I chuckled.

"Well, well. Just what do you think you're doing, Mr. Lightwood?"

He placed a few more kisses along my neck and jaw before answering, "A man has the right to enjoy when his wife looks particularly beautiful, doesn't he? Besides, I would like to enjoy seeing you like this now in case Washington decides that you should dress like a man again. I won't be able to kiss you then, so I should take my fill while I am able."

I chuckled again, turning my head to allow his mouth to find mine. His tongue slowly stroked across mine, stoking a fire low inside me.

When the downstairs clock chimed five, Gracen reluctantly pulled away. "Come on, let's go."

I groaned. "Do we have to?"

Gracen's only answer was to give me a quick kiss on the mouth and then take my hand.

When we arrived downstairs for dinner, Titus informed us that dinner would be slightly delayed, the expression on his face clearly saying that there was a reason he wasn't going to share. I banished his smirk from my mind as Gracen and I made our way toward the library, planning to spend a few more precious minutes alone while we waited.

Except we weren't alone. Standing in the middle of the one room where I'd felt comfortable was the person I despised more than Roston.

"Well, Gracen, Honor. Welcome back."

"Clara?" Gracen asked, "what are you doing here?"

She smiled that sickly sweet smile of hers. "It would have been terribly rude for me to ignore your homecoming. I had to come by and welcome you both back."

"We were gone for scarcely three days," I pointed out, not bothering to play nice with my tone. Clara already knew that I despised her, so why should I try to hide it?

She continued to smile, tilting her head in a way that made her sandy hair catch the flickering lamplight. She also completely ignored my statement and went on with whatever it was she'd come here to say.

"I've been ever so busy as of late. Quincy and I have been seeing quite a lot of each other, and he wishes me to accompany him to so many functions, I can hardly find time to do anything else. It's just been so exhausting." She laughed in the most irritatingly artificial way.

It set my teeth on edge.

"Oh, the trials of the upper class," I said, my voice dripping with mock sympathy.

I felt Gracen press my arm, and I took a mental step back. Though I saw no reason to act civil with this woman, I would try to control myself for his sake.

At least, Gracen didn't make me say anything else. "Thank you for taking the time out of your busy schedule to make an appearance, but please feel free to return to your obligations now that you've welcomed my wife and me home."

I tried not to look smug about both his dismissal and his not-so-subtle reminder of who I was to him.

Clara tossed a silky lock of hair over her shoulder and took a few steps toward the window, a far-off look coming over her face. "I suppose I should return now. Quincy and I do hate to be apart.

We've become very fond of each other, you know."

I almost snorted. They hardly knew each other. This was a ploy to make Gracen jealous. Any idiot could see it. But it didn't matter. She could try all she wanted, but it wouldn't make a difference. I just wondered if she had herself convinced with any of this shit.

"Then you mustn't keep him waiting," Gracen said.

Clara looked at the two of us for a long time, her perfectly formed lips twisting into a scowl. "If you're sure that's what you want." She paused, her scowl deepening when she realized Gracen wasn't going to try to stop her.

With an overdramatic flounce, Clara hurried out, slamming the door behind her.

"Sore loser," I said.

Gracen looked confused by my words, reminding me that the expression wasn't exactly commonplace in this particular time.

"She's jealous," I clarified. "Because I got you and she didn't."

He shook his head. "It seems petty after our meeting with Washington, doesn't it? So many more important things to worry about."

I nodded. "Do you think he'll contact us about joining?"

Gracen shrugged. "I believe that if he believes it will be beneficial to the cause, he will."

I reached out and took his hand. "I'm so sorry that I've made things so hard for you."

He gave me an exasperated smile. "I love you so much, and even more so due to your understanding. I don't know where I would be if you weren't here with me."

I put my hand on his face. "Gracen, are you sure about this?"

He leaned into my touch. "Honor. I do believe that the people who have come to call this land home have a right to govern it however they see fit. *That* is the reason I agree with you. We will fight for our right to choose how to live our lives."

The tension in me eased at his words. As long as we both knew where we stood, we could do this. We *would* do this.

Chapter 11

When a third week had passed and there was still no word from Washington, I began to feel restless, a strange sort of discontent that came with not having a purpose. It was that purposelessness that I'd dreaded when I tried to decide whether or not I wanted to re-enlist, and the fact that I'd found it here wasn't sitting well with me. It didn't help that Roston's attitude toward us was as cold as ever, though he seemed to avoid both Gracen and me. I could tell it hurt Gracen, but I couldn't help thinking it was actually better than the alternative.

While there was plenty of room on the estate for us to co-exist, it wasn't exactly comfortable for either of us, but I knew that our best bet was to stay here. Aside from the fact that we needed Washington to be able to find us if he needed us, the best way for us to pick up on any new information from the Loyalists was to be around them. If we left, we'd be losing the very thing that would make us an asset to the cause.

Which meant, at least until we received other instructions, we were staying right here.

I wrung the excess water from my hair and wrapped a towel around me as I stepped out of the tub. It took so long to carry and heat enough water to fill a tub that I only got a real bath every couple days. The rest of the time, it was a general wash up from a basin which, in the middle of August, didn't really get one feeling very fresh.

Gracen's lips brushed my shoulder as he came to stand behind me. "Could you please tell me how you manage to be like this every day?"

I looked up at him, eyebrow raised. "What's that supposed to mean?" My tone was teasing so he wouldn't take the question the wrong way.

He smiled, his eyes dancing. "Tell me how you manage to look so beautiful all the time."

I rolled my eyes. "Gracen, seriously, if you wanted sex, you don't have to bother with sweet talk."

He laughed, but it was the low sort of chuckle that made me press my thighs together. He ran his hand over my shoulder, up my neck, and cupped the side of my face. His thumb brushed against the corner of my mouth, and he bent his head to touch his lips to mine in a chaste but sweet kiss.

When he pulled back, he rested his forehead against mine. "I need you to know that I love you, Honor Lightwood, and that I want you by my side today, tomorrow, and twenty, fifty years from now."

I may have told him that I didn't need sweet talk, but that didn't mean his words didn't make me choke up. "I love you too, Gracen, and I don't intend to go anywhere. I wouldn't be shocked if you actually get a bit bored of me one day."

"I would never." His eyes shone in the warm sunlight filtering through the windows, and I couldn't help but kiss him one more time before we each had to tend to the events of the day.

Even though I'd been expecting it for a few weeks now, the headline still came as a bit of a shock.

King George Issues Proclamation of Rebellion.

It happened a month ago, like I originally thought, but I hadn't taken into account how long it took information to get from one country to the other. Now, it was nearing the end of September, and we were finally receiving the official word of the proclamation.

"Gracen, look at this," I said as I carried the paper into our bedroom.

He turned away from the wash basin, drying his jaw with a towel as his eyes scanned the front page.

"My god, it's starting," he murmured.

"What do you think your father will say about this?" I couldn't help but ask.

Gracen ran his hand through his hair. "I'm unsure, but I doubt it will be anything good."

I crossed over to him, tossing the paper onto the bed. His expression was troubled, and all thoughts of war and everything else went right out the window. All I cared about was getting that look off his face.

"Hey, remember what we said?" I took his hands in mine. "We're in this together."

He nodded and kissed my forehead, his fingers tightening around mine. "I know." He wrapped his arms around me, pulling me against his chest. "Washington will send word now. He'll want inside information."

I nodded as my pulse skipped a beat. It was really happening. I'd been considering leaving the army in my own time, becoming a civilian and staying away from war, and now I was in a whole different century...and becoming a part of another war. At least, this time, I knew when and how it would end.

It still didn't make it any easier as Gracen and I went through the motions around the estate. We continued to avoid Roston – or he avoided us – but I still felt like I was on edge. I'd never thought of myself as impatient, but this waiting was driving me crazy. At least in the army, I had specific routines to follow to keep me focused.

Here, however, I did have one thing I didn't have in the army.

Sex.

With my smoking hot husband.

Orgasms were a great distraction, I decided as Gracen and I lay next to each other in the slowly lightening room. We'd both woken before dawn, though perhaps woken wasn't the right word since neither of us had actually slept last night. Dozed on and off, but not slept.

I wasn't entirely sure which of us had technically started things, only that absent caresses had turned into something else while the sky was still dark. The whisper of sheets on skin, the early autumn sounds had surrounded us, and neither of us had felt the need to break it.

He'd moved over me, slid inside me with ease, his way slicked by the preparation his fingers and tongue had done. We'd taken our time, making love slowly until we came together, and now we were simply basking in the afterglow, lying comfortably together as we waited for the rest of the household to stir.

"May I ask you something about your life...before?" Gracen's fingers were tracing a pattern on my skin, and they hesitated as he spoke, piquing my curiosity.

"Go for it."

"When did your husband pass?"

I lifted my head to look at him, the room light enough now for me to see his face. "My husband?"

"When we..." A flush crept up his neck. "You said you had been...intimate before. I believe you called him Bruce."

I nodded, still trying to understand why he thought I'd been married and widowed. Then it hit me – he assumed that since I'd experienced intimacy with a man, we must have been married. And that since I hadn't referred to myself as still being married when I came here, I must've been widowed. Other people during this time period might not have thought of a servant sleeping with the master of a house as being *too* unconventional, but a respectable woman surely wouldn't have, and he assumed I was respectable.

"Things are different in the time I come from," I said carefully. "People are less strict about saving intimacy for marriage."

Gracen's face went blank, making it impossible to read what he was thinking. "You were never married?"

"I was engaged to be married." I didn't think it was a good idea to tell him that Bruce and I had slept together before we'd gotten engaged. As it was, I was wondering if it would've been better to have lied.

"But you never exchanged vows."

I pushed myself up, not bothering to cover my breasts as the sheet fell. "No. We didn't."

He sat up, turning away from me as he muttered something that didn't sound very nice.

I stood, needing the distance as my stomach churned. "You're angry?"

"Of course I'm angry," he snapped.

"Are you kidding me?" I struggled to keep my voice down. "You and I had sex before we got married. In fact, we hadn't even known each other that long. Bruce and I had been together since we were kids."

"That's not the point," Gracen said as he pulled on his nightshirt and a pair of pants.

"Oh, it isn't? You're a fucking hypocrite. I was out of my time, out of my world. You knew what the expectations of this time were and you did it anyway. I had no expectations of you, no expectations for us, but that was my choice. You don't get to shame me when you made the same choice even though you knew what it meant here."

"It's not the same thing." Gracen was pacing now, but he wouldn't look at me.

"Why? Because I'm a woman? So it's okay for me to put my life on the line in my time and this one, but I'm a slut because I slept with a man I intended to marry in a time when most women my age have had several sexual partners."

"It's a matter of principle, Honor."

"A matter of principle? Bullshit! You were engaged to Clara when we slept together. How the hell is that more *principled* than what I did before I even met you?"

He moved toward the door. "It seems there is still much about your past that I don't know."

It's the future actually, I thought, *but let's not be particular about the details, shall we?*

A few moments of terrible silence hung in the air before he continued, "The situation at hand is an important one, and it deserves our undivided attention. I don't believe I can properly focus while wondering what you're hiding from me. Full trust is imperative if we are to serve Washington together, and I obviously haven't warranted that."

With those words, he turned and left the room.

I stood, staring at the door as it closed behind him. What the hell just happened?

Chapter 12

When Gracen walked out, saying that we had mistrust between us, I assumed he'd spend some time going around the estate, getting his head together before coming back in. Maybe he'd be gone most of the day, returning only for dinner and then a returned to our discussion with a cooler head. I hadn't, for one moment, imagined that when I arrived in the kitchen after two hours of tossing and turning, Dye would be waiting for me.

"Master Gracen had himself leavin' in a hurry," she said, her tone casual, though the look in her eyes was anything but.

I froze, my stomach sinking even as I told myself not to jump to any conclusions. "Leaving?"

Dye nodded as she finished emptying the bucket of water. "He come down here, looking all bothered about somethin' and grabbed dat salted beef Cook been saving, then headed to the barn." She leaned closer, dropping her voice. "I seen him ride outta there like the devil hisself was after him."

I leaned heavily against the table, the strength running out of my legs. Gracen had left on a horse, which meant he'd felt the need to get farther and faster away than he could get on foot.

Then the rest of what she said clicked, and the

blood drained from my face.

"Dye." My voice was little more than a whisper. "How much food did he take?"

The slight pause before her answer told me that she'd figured out why I asked. "Nuff for at least two days travel."

"Fuck, Gracen," I breathed the words as I closed my eyes.

I let myself have a few moments to hurt, to be angry at Gracen for running, then I took a deep breath and set about figuring out what I should do now.

The answer was as problematic as it was clear.

I had to go after him, force him to have it out with me so I could know if I'd made a mistake choosing him. I hated the thought of it, but it was better to find out now than later...like when I got pregnant.

And I was pretty sure it'd be a *when* not an *if*.

But I didn't want to think about that now. I had to get to him.

Once I made myself think logically, I knew where he'd gone, and where I had to go. I didn't let myself think about how dangerous this was, or what could happen with a single misstep. The memory of that Bradbury short story about the guy who stepped on a butterfly in the past and destroyed his world kept circling in my head as I threw together some clothes, some provisions, and took Gracen's remaining horse.

As I rode out, I prayed that Washington hadn't changed his camp's location...and that I wasn't too late.

I was tired, dirty, and starting to question just how much I was willing to take before I decided that I'd made a mistake. I'd wanted to ride all night, but no matter how tough I was, I wasn't used to being on a horse for such an extended period of time, and I needed to rest. Still, I pushed myself as far and fast as I could, and now I was finally at the perimeter of the camp.

I climbed off the horse, mentally cursing my dress for the millionth time. I needed to be recognizable when I arrived, so I hadn't changed into pants, no matter how much the outfit was pissing me off.

"Can I help you, Miss?" The sentry's voice was polite but firm.

"I need to see Gracen Lightwood."

No recognition registered on the man's face. In fact, his expression didn't change at all.

"Gracen Lightwood," I repeated impatiently. "Is he here? He would have arrived yesterday sometime, looking for General Washington. We were here together before."

"Miss, I think you need to get back on that horse and go back to wherever it is you came from."

I stood my ground. "Tell me where my husband is."

The sentry sighed. "I don't know of a Gracen Lightwood...but, General Washington is in the tent speaking with some of his advisors. Maybe he can help you."

For the first time since I'd arrived here, I was grateful for the way most men viewed women. If we'd been with my unit in my time, no one would've gotten through to a commanding officer so easily, not even a woman.

"Take me to him." I hadn't been a commanding officer, but I knew how to speak with authority, so I did.

The man nodded, and I followed him through the camp, keeping my chin up and my eyes straight ahead. I could feel soldiers looking at me, but none of them were Gracen, so I didn't care. I was grateful for my guide, as the way was vaguely familiar, but not so much so that I would've been able to locate Washington's tent on my own.

"Sir, there's a Mrs. Lightwood here, seeking her husband. She said she met with you recently."

A muffled reply came from inside, and then the soldier was motioning for me to follow.

"Give us a moment, gentlemen," Washington said to the others as he came around the desk to shake my hand.

The other men murmured their farewells to Washington, as well as acknowledgments to me, as they exited. Washington gestured toward a chair, and I took it, watching as he sat next to me. Now that I was here, I realized I hadn't thought this far ahead. I hadn't considered what I'd do if Gracen wasn't here and I had to talk to Washington alone.

"Mrs. Lightwood, I wasn't expecting to see you here."

I decided that straightforward was the best approach under the circumstances. I needed to find my husband, and niceties wouldn't help in that regard. "General Washington, is Gracen here?"

Washington didn't seem at all offended by my crazed demand and lack of respect. If anything, I got the impression that he rather liked my blunt manner.

"He was here," Washington said, gesturing toward a cup a soldier had brought in without me noticing.

I didn't reach for the drink, no matter how thirsty I was. I had more pressing matters on my mind. "Where is he?"

Washington took the cup and set it on his desk. "Gracen asked to be given an immediate assignment now that the king has issued the proclamation you predicted. As I am not in a position to turn away an able-bodied man, I commissioned him to help rally support in France. The Marquis de Lafayette has been a great help, and I hope that your husband will be able to recruit more than him."

France. My heart gave an unsteady thump. Washington had sent my husband to France.

I gripped my hands together tight enough to make my knuckles turn white. "I need to see him."

Washington placed a hand on my shoulder. I realized only then that it was because I'd swayed slightly. I'd eaten less than I'd slept, and I was running on fumes. I couldn't stop though. Not until I saw Gracen.

"He's not here," Washington said gently. "He's waiting to board a ship."

Waiting. The word sparked in my brain. "When does he leave?"

"The ship departs in two days." He paused, then added, "I can make arrangements for you to see him before they set sail. After you eat and rest."

I started to protest, but Washington's expression

was firm.

"You will fall off your horse if you go like this. It's a journey of a few hours. Eat. Sleep. And then I will have a letter for you at first light, so none of my men will stop you."

I found myself so physically and emotionally tired that I didn't have the energy to refuse. I barely remember following Washington out of his tent and being led to an empty one. He said he'd have someone bring me a meal, but the moment he left, I collapsed into a deep sleep.

I woke with a now familiar feeling of disorientation, but still feeling far more capable than when I'd drifted off. There was a plate of food sitting by the bed, containing the usual army staple of the time: hardtack and dried meat. Hardly appetizing, but my growling stomach didn't care. I recalled that Washington had promised a letter for safe passage to Gracen, and that was all that mattered.

The camp was full of organized chaos, and I couldn't help but notice the similarities to the army in my own time. The uniforms were different, and the lack of technology was obvious, but these were still the same sort of men I'd spent the last six years around.

The soldier who'd been guarding my tent – whether out of chivalry or suspicion, I didn't know – escorted me back to Washington, staying outside while I entered the tent. The cool morning air, along with food and rest, had cleared my head and given me a better grip on my emotions, so I was able to face the general with a smile, and a refreshed determination.

He greeted me with a smile. "Were you able to sleep?"

"Yes, Sir. I thank you for the accommodations as well as the food."

"I am only sorry we had such poor fare to offer."

He gestured toward the same seat I'd taken last night. Despite my eagerness to get to Gracen, I knew I needed to hear whatever Washington had to say. Mine and Gracen's presence was messing with the timeline enough as it was. I couldn't risk the future of an entire country for selfish purposes. Not any more than I already was.

"Your prediction of the king's declaration was correct." The general's voice was even, his expression inscrutable. "Some of my men would regard such intuition as suspicious, but I believe I have a soldier's instincts, and those instincts tell me that you are trustworthy."

I chose my own words carefully, understanding the importance of not trying too hard. "Does this mean you want my assistance?"

Washington nodded. "A man doesn't always need to understand something in order to utilize it," he said, chuckling wryly.

I smiled. "I thank you for your trust, and I'll do my best to prove myself worthy of it." I paused and then asked, "This trip to France. Will it be...dangerous, do you think?"

Washington's hesitation told me he was considering how honest to be. "I cannot say how perilous it'll be, but no one is truly safe from danger while we are at war. Anyone who's committed to the cause must be prepared to accept that."

"That's what makes you such a great leader," I said. "The people know that you're willing to risk it all too, that's why they trust you to lead."

He gave me a strange look, and I suddenly remembered that even though he'd been appointed the commander of the Continental Army, he hadn't been particularly popular, especially this early in the war. Despite becoming the first president, he'd been a soldier more than a politician.

"Is that so?" His gaze was searching as he stood.

I could have blown it off, made some sort of excuse for what I'd said, but I didn't know what that would do to history. Besides, how would someone tell *George Washington* that they hadn't meant to say that people would trust him to lead?

"Yes, Sir." I met his eyes. "You have so many great things in your future."

The silence between us held for several long seconds before he broke it. "Your horse has been fed and watered." He picked up a piece of paper from his desk and handed it to me. "Here is your pass. Be careful."

I took the paper and tucked it into the front of my dress. "Thank you, General."

He smiled again. "I truly hope your husband knows how fortunate he is to have a wife who loves him as you do."

I hoped so too.

Chapter 13

Even though I'd reminded myself half a dozen times that the ship wasn't set to sail for another thirteen hours, I wanted to push my horse to the limit. Only the knowledge that it'd harm the animal kept me in check. I'd certainly taken modern transportation for granted. Need to be halfway across the country by this afternoon? Here's a plane ticket to get you there in time for dinner, no problem. Want to go from Philadelphia to New York City? Less than three hours unless traffic was a real bitch. The distance I had to travel now would've been an hour with a Mazda at my disposal.

When I finally reached the settlement boarding the dock, my nerves were stretched taut, frayed by the hours on horseback spent worrying about what I would do if I didn't reach him in time. I stopped at the edge of the crowd, taking advantage of being higher than the throngs of sailors teeming about to scan the crowd for Gracen. He could've been inside for all I knew, but I had to start somewhere.

I skimmed over the men with the wrong color hair, eyes flicking across features and builds, immediately dismissing those who didn't fit. I knew his body well enough to know just by the way men moved that they weren't him.

Then I saw him, and my breath caught in my throat. He was assisting a line of men in loading supplies onto a wagon that was headed to the ship, his back to me. I stayed where I was, watching him. Sweat drenched his loose-fitting shirt, darkened his wild waves. He looked like he was so busy, I wondered if he'd been thinking of me half as much as I'd been thinking of him, and the thought that he hadn't made my heart clench painfully.

It was that need to know that got me off the horse. I tossed the reins over the closest post, barely paying enough attention to make sure the horse wouldn't get loose.

I pushed my way through the crowd, making it within a couple feet before Gracen looked up and noticed me. He stopped working as our eyes locked. Without looking away, he said a quick word to one of the men near him, then closed the distance between us in a few long strides.

I'd expected him to hesitate, but he pulled me straight into his arms, burying his face in the crook of my neck.

"I'm sorry," I said, the words muffled against his chest. "I should've been clearer about my past."

Gracen leaned back, already shaking his head. "You have no need to be sorry, darling. I had no right to say any of those things. You have more integrity and honor than any person I have ever known, and I was wrong to have judged you by a standard held two hundred years before you were born. Especially when I applied it to you and not myself." He cupped my face, brushing his thumbs against the corners of my mouth. "Forgive me, my love. I hated the thought of any other man having had you."

His mouth brushed across mine, then came down more firmly, tongue teasing the seam of my mouth for a moment before sliding between my lips. He kissed me slowly, deeply, not caring who saw or what he was supposed to have been doing. He showed me without additional words how sorry he was for what happened between us, and I responded in kind, letting him know that he was forgiven.

"I came as soon as I could," I told him when I could breathe again. I stroked his cheek with my fingers, the pain I'd felt during his absence somehow turning more acute now that I could touch him...and knew he was supposed to be leaving with the morning tide.

"You're here now. That is all that matters." He wrapped his arms around me and pulled me close.

"Let me come with you," I said as I smoothed my hands up and down his back. "This isn't how it was supposed to go. We were supposed to do this together. How can we do that if you're across the ocean?"

"No."

The word was harsh, and I stiffened, tried to take a step back. His embrace tightened, keeping me in place.

"Not for the reasons I know you are thinking." His tone softened. "I could never live with myself if something happened to you. I know that you can handle yourself, but I do not think I can concentrate on what I need to do if I don't know you are here, as safe as you can be." He buried his face in my hair, taking a deep breath. "I cannot do it. I need you here though Washington needs me elsewhere."

I wanted to argue with him, tell him that the safest and best place for me to be was at his side, but

I knew this wasn't the time or the place to have that talk. We didn't have a lot of time, but we had some.

"Come with me," he said quietly as he laced his fingers between mine.

I let him lead me through the people, past the sailors and the merchants, past his horse as he tossed a coin to a nearby boy and gave instructions to take it to the stable where his other horse was. All this I barely registered, so focused was I on the solid feel of his hand in mine. I didn't realize that we were at an inn until he took me past the tables on the main floor to the stairs.

"I was fortunate they had a room," he said as he opened a door to a room barely half the size of the one we'd shared back at the Lightwood estate.

"Why didn't you just stay with the soldiers?" I asked.

"If I'm to play the part of a Loyalist so I can gather information for Washington, the last place anyone should see me is with the Continental Army."

I hadn't thought of that. It made sense now why Washington hadn't offered to send a soldier with me. I hadn't really given it much thought at the time, but now I realized it was strange that he'd been okay with me traveling on my own.

Gracen leaned down and nuzzled the spot under my ear as his fingers started pulling at my dress. "And I am even more grateful now to have a private room."

So was I.

I needed him. Needed to feel him touching me, inside me.

Suddenly, I was glad that I hadn't put on all those layers because my dress was sliding off and his hands were pulling up my shift, palms hot on my bare skin. I yanked his shirt over his head, our limbs tangling as he tried to rid me of the last of my clothing. The tension between us shifted as we fell onto the bed, mouths and hands desperate, urgent.

His knee slid between mine as he leaned down to flick his tongue across the tip of my nipple. I ran my hands down his back and tried to forget that it would be months before I'd feel his body above mine. He was here with me now, and that was all that mattered at the moment.

"Touch me," I murmured against his mouth. "Please, Gracen. Touch me."

His eyes darkened as his hand moved between us, fingers slipping over my clit. I moaned, arching up into his touch.

"I love when you do that." His voice was low, rough. "I love that I can make you do that."

"More." I grabbed at his arms, nails digging into his skin. "*More.*"

He smiled that slow, seductive smile that made my insides go all gooey...then he pushed two fingers inside me.

I cried out, my eyes rolling back in my head at the little spark of pain that came with the pleasure of being stretched. I wasn't into the hardcore S&M kind of stuff like spanking, but a little rough edge to things...damn it felt good. I knew Gracen had been holding back, even when I'd told him that I wanted him harder or faster, but what happened between us recently had loosened something.

"Make me come," I begged. "Please, Gracen."

He sucked hard on my nipple, using his teeth on the sensitive skin as he drove his fingers into me until I came apart in his arms. I expected to feel him sliding into me, but instead, he moved down my body, settling between my legs.

"Fuck!" I couldn't stop myself from shouting as he gave me a long, slow lick.

If I'd known he planned on going down on me, I would've told him not to, not before I'd had the chance to bathe. But he didn't seem to mind, and as he used his thumbs to open me to his questing tongue, I forgot why I was supposed to care.

I writhed against his mouth, whimpering as he teased me. He was taking his time, exploring every inch of me, and I lost track of where we were and what awaited us. My world was sensation and sound. My own moans and the soft murmurs of inaudible words against my flesh. The rough quilt beneath my back. His silky hair between my fingers.

And the incredible, white-hot pleasure of an impossible, never-ending orgasm.

When he finally buried himself inside me with one smooth thrust, every cell in my body felt electrified. Each stroke sent me further and higher, racing with Gracen toward the inevitable end. It was hearing my name on his lips when he finally reached his climax that sent me tipping over the edge to mine.

I watched Gracen from between half-open lids as he propped himself up on one elbow, stroking my temple with his fingertips. I couldn't bring myself to risk looking at him fully, not while I could feel the moisture burning to escape. He was being far more honorable than myself, going where he was needed, even if it meant giving up what he wanted. I knew it was selfish to not want him to go, but I didn't care. I'd been so prepared to fight together, and now I felt alone in a world and space that weren't my own.

He took my face in his hands, forcing me to look straight at him. The tears spilled over as I stared up at the face that had become my world, my everything.

"I can't lose you," I choked out.

"You won't." Gracen meant to be reassuring, but I knew that he was thinking of the same thing I was. Though I knew what the outcome of the big events ahead of us would be, I didn't know if we would both make it out of this turning point in history alive, *together*. I knew American history, but I didn't know our future.

He kissed me deeply, his body pressed against mine so that I could feel every hard line of him. I tasted the salt of tears on my lips but didn't know if they were mine or his. My body ached with the memory of having him inside me, ached with the knowledge that it could have been the last time.

It was strange. I'd said goodbye to family and friends, to a fiancé, when I'd deployed overseas. Six years of being in the military and never knowing if I was saying goodbye for the last time, I should've been used to tearless farewells and the pang of departure. But with Gracen it was different. I felt like I was losing a piece of myself. Like he was taking something deep and vital with him.

As he reluctantly pulled away, I curled on my side, my cheek pressed against the flat pillow, watching him wash, then dress. When he had his pants and shirt on, he turned back to me, tying back his cuffs as he crossed to the bed. Unlike the clothes he'd worn yesterday to help the sailors, he had more formal attire on now. Dressing the part of the relatively wealthy Loyalist.

"You need to get dressed if you're going to see me off," he said. "The tide waits for no one."

"I can't, Gracen," I answered, hot tears rolling down my cheeks. "I can't watch you leave."

He knelt so that his gaze was level with mine, his eyes reflecting the pain I felt. "Even if we're not physically in the same place, we're still doing this together. Please, my love. I want to have your face as the last thing left in my mind as I go."

Shit. How could I deny him that? He'd given up so much for me, meant so much to me. I had to go. It had never been this difficult for me to part with Bruce, and it certainly hadn't been this grievous for my former fiancé to see me off. All the more confirmation that what I'd felt for Bruce hadn't been real love. Gracen was my other half, my soulmate. All the things I'd never believed in until I met him.

I dragged myself out of bed, reveling in each twinge that reminded me of the depths of the passion we'd shared last night. Even though I knew this would be the hardest thing I'd ever had to do, I washed up and dressed, putting on the best of the dresses I'd brought with me. It wasn't much, but it was enough to keep his cover.

Hand-in-hand, we made our way to the ship, neither one of us speaking. Soldiers were hard at work up and down the docks, loading up the last of supplies, shouting orders and greetings to one another. The absence of soldiers from either army made me uneasy as I realized I didn't know much of anything about what had happened on the shores and seas during the war. The Boston Tea Party, obviously, but even as I racked my brains, I couldn't think of anything that would reassure me to the safety of my husband.

My body almost resisted his touch when he reached for me because I knew that this was it, and every one of my senses rebelled against the very thought. I knew that this was as painful for him as it was for me, and neither of us was strong enough to turn down what could be a final embrace. I clung to him as he kissed me, pouring every ounce of love and desire into that single moment, and feeling it in return.

Gracen pressed one last kiss to my forehead before turning swiftly away. I covered my mouth to keep from sobbing audibly, but inside I had already broken down. I watched Gracen's broad back as he made his way to the ship, slipping through my fingers with every step, taking my heart with him as he went.

Chapter 14

I was about to retreat back to the inn to cry before making plans of what to do next, when suddenly, I realized something. I looked just like one of those young sailors when I first arrived here. Hadn't even Gracen mistaken me for a young man at first? I'd fooled him for far longer than even I had expected. Surely I could do it again...perhaps even long enough to make it to the open sea where there would be no choice but to take me along.

I told myself it was a bad idea, that Gracen's reasons for leaving me behind had made sense. That I could put the ship at risk by adding an extra mouth to feed on a journey that would take at least a month. But none of that outweighed the thought of spending months, maybe years, without Gracen. It was the possibility of losing him forever, and maybe never even knowing it, that got me moving.

I'd only brought a dress with me, having left my twenty-first-century uniform hidden under a loose floorboard back in our room at the estate, so if I was going to do this, I needed to find clothes, and fast. As I looked around, I spotted an unattended bag lying close by. Before I could talk myself out of it, I made my way toward it as inconspicuously as I could.

I felt bad for stealing, but desperate times called for desperate measures. I pushed aside the guilt as I slipped into a nearby shed and changed my clothes. The minutes seemed to fly by as my shaking fingers struggled with all the ties and loops that imprisoned me in swathes of fabric. My heart was racing as I shoved my things into the now empty bag. I needed to have a dress for when we arrived in France, if for no other reason than to not make a scene. The mission was too important.

I pulled my hair back into the low ponytail men of this time sported, took a deep breath, and then stepped back out into the sunlight. I forced myself not to run, choosing a brisk pace that wouldn't attract much attention. When I passed the place where I found the bag, I dropped my small bag of coins and hoped that they'd find their way into the hands of the person whose clothes I'd taken.

I didn't let myself dwell on the guilt though. I had to get to the ship, or the entire thing would've been pointless. To my relief, I saw one of the sailors shouting at a few men who appeared to be staggering toward the ramp. I glanced around as I slid into place behind them, avoiding eye contact with anyone who might recognize me. Fortunately, most of the men were far too occupied with preparations of setting sail to pay me much attention as I followed the stragglers onto the deck.

I ducked into a dark corner and watched, waiting to see what happened next. My heart leapt into my throat a moment later as Gracen came around the corner, deep in conversation with one of the sailors. I knew I needed to stay out of sight until we were well into the voyage. They couldn't very well turn around just to put one lone woman back where she belonged, could they? With that in mind, I sunk deeper into the shadows, searching for the most discreet way to sneak below deck where I could find a place to remain hidden for as long as possible. I wasn't going to take any chances.

I jolted awake when the ship rocked beneath me. I'd drifted off a couple of hours ago, the stress and emotional toll of the last few days draining me to the point of exhaustion. I rubbed my eyes, flinching at a sharp pain going through my lower back as I moved. I massaged the knot of muscle with my fist, pulling myself to an upright position before stumbling to my feet. The motion of the vessel made me feel queasy, and I hoped that I'd adjust quickly. The last thing I needed was to be seasick on a month-long voyage with a sure-to-be-pissed husband.

I had no way of telling how far we'd come, but the little I knew about tides made me think that as long as we were on our way, I'd be safe. It wasn't like in my time where a motor could work against a current. Even if the ship had rowers, I doubted the captain would want to waste the energy just to drop me off. I did, however, need to get some fresh air. Seeing what time of day it was would also help orient me.

I made my way out of the depths of the boat, breathing in the fresh air gratefully the moment I stepped out onto the deck. I saw a few sailors milling about, but it was clear this wasn't a passenger vessel any more than it was a military one. I wasn't sure if that boded good or bad for me, but it was too late to change my mind.

I stayed in the shadows as I took slow, deep draughts of the briny air, shivering at the chill. It was already dark, but not so much so that I thought it too late. The stars seemed to be only just coming out, the sky still holding that purplish hue that made me think it wasn't quite midnight yet. I'd slept longer than I realized. The fact that no one had noticed me meant that my little nook behind the barrels of provisions would be safe, at least for now. I wanted to wait at least until morning before I revealed myself to Gracen. He was going to be furious with me, but I knew it'd be better to do things that way rather than risk him finding out by accident.

Once I'd breathed in as much fresh air as I could hold, I went back below, hoping I could still remain undiscovered until morning. As I settled myself back into the tight space, I told myself that no matter what Gracen thought, I needed to be with him. I could be a valuable asset, though my knowledge of what happened on the French side of things was limited to the name Lafayette. If nothing else, being at his side would give me peace of mind, and I'd argue that, in the long run, it'd be easier for him as well. After all, at least he could keep an eye on me in France and not wonder about what sorts of trouble I was getting myself into.

I fell asleep to the sound of water lapping against the sides of the ship, my head full of the possibilities that awaited our arrival on French shores.

I woke up at an unknown hour, my heart pounding, skin slick with sweat despite the chill. I couldn't remember what I'd dreamed, but the sense of fear and sorrow was unmistakable, as was the knowledge of who it was about.

Gracen.

I needed to see him. Needed to reassure myself that he was okay.

It was dark, and I had no idea where I was going, but I tiptoed my way across the pitching floorboards. I didn't know if Gracen had a cabin or if he was sleeping with the crew, but my sleep-addled brain knew that there were only so many places he could be, so I'd find him eventually.

To my surprise, after only a couple minutes, I almost stumbled over him as I tried to find the steps up to the deck. His hammock hung low from the ceiling, the only one in this part of the ship. Judging by the sounds and smells coming from somewhere to my right, some of the crew bunked down here too, but he was the only one I cared about.

When it came to my husband, I had a bad habit of acting without thinking, and this time was no different. I leaned down and pressed my lips against his forehead. A moment later, he jerked awake, expression startled...then his eyes narrowed.

"Honor?" he whispered as he sat up. "What are

you doing here?"

"I couldn't do it," I confessed, moving back so that he could stand.

As soon as he was on his feet, he took my face in his hands, his eyes searching mine, as if waiting for me to admit that I'm crazy. "What were you thinking?"

I tried not to be hurt by the harsh quality of his voice. "I was thinking that I didn't want to lose you."

"This is no place for you," he said as if I hadn't even spoken. "On a ship, with a bunch of men, on our way to try to negotiate with people who may or may not support our cause. And if we make a single misstep, we could end up in prison...or worse."

I tried not to be insulted. "I have a bit of experience being surrounded by men...and holding my own, Gracen. I was a soldier, and a damn good one."

His jaw tightened, and if it wasn't for the concern I could see even in the dim light, I would've been pissed. As it was, I was still annoyed.

"What am I going to do with you?" The question was quiet, but not soft.

"Nothing," I snapped. "This was clearly a mistake. So just ignore me, and I'll make my own way."

He glared at me. "Why are you making this so difficult?"

"We planned to do this together from the start, and now that I'm here, you don't want me."

"I'm trying to *protect* you, Honor. Just because you were a soldier in your time does not mean you can be a soldier here and now."

I tried not to be offended by the fact that he didn't want me with him. After all, I understood wanting to keep the person I loved safe. But, this was war, and if we were going to do what was right, we couldn't try to shelter each other. I did, however, need to accept that he felt responsible for me. It was part of being married, especially in a time where the traditional roles of husband and wife were the norm instead of something old-fashioned.

I took a slow breath and softened my tone. "I know that you want to keep me safe, but I want us to do this together. Side by side. I feel that that's how it's meant to be. From the very first day. Isn't it how we escaped from the enemy camp? Even from your father?"

He sighed, reaching out to place his palm against the side of my face. "I wish you had listened to me. I knew you were safe there."

I raised an eyebrow. "Safe? In a country that's at war?" A wave of insecurity washed over me, and I started to turn away. "If you just didn't want me to come with you—"

His hand closed around my arm, and he pulled me around to face him again. "I always want you with me."

I kissed his chin, a smile playing on my lips. "I should still apologize."

He gave me a puzzled look that made me laugh, and I took his hand, pulling him after me as I led the way back to the corner where I'd been hiding. Since he clearly didn't have a private room, this would have to do, because I sure as hell wasn't waiting a month to give him a proper...apology.

"Honor!" Gracen couldn't hold in his surprise as I pushed him against the wall and went down onto my knees in front of him. "What are you—?"

The sentence ended on a groan as I palmed him

through his pants. I looked up at him, watching his breathing quicken as I undid his breeches and reached inside. He made a strangled sound as I flicked my tongue across the tip of him. He was only half-hard, but I knew it wouldn't take much to get him all the way up. I hadn't asked him directly, but I was still pretty sure that blowjobs were a novelty.

"Shh," I murmured. "I'm going to need you to be very quiet, Mr. Lightwood."

I squeezed him hard enough to make him swear, but not so much that it would actually hurt.

"Quieter than that," I said. I ran my tongue around him, easing the friction my hand created. "Unless, of course, you want all of those sailors back there waking up and investigating."

I used my tongue on him a bit more, teasing, caressing. I let his head slip between my lips, felt him swell and thicken as I applied steady suction.

"Honor," he moaned my name, his hand dropping to my head, fingers tightening in my hair.

I let his cock slide from my mouth with a near-obscene sound. "Do you want them to look over here?" I asked as I kept my hand moving. "See you with your cock in someone's mouth? I'd love to watch you explain this to them."

"I want..."

Even in the darkness, I could see the heat suffuse his face.

"What do you want, *my love*?" I used his term of endearment. "Tell me what you want."

"Your mouth. Please, Honor."

The moment I took him back into my mouth, his head fell back against the wall with a thunk. As much as I would've liked to torture him, drag it out until he was begging for release, I knew that would've been taking the risk too far.

So I used every trick I knew to take him straight to climax, ignoring the sting in my scalp as he pulled my hair. His thigh muscles bunched and jumped under my hands, and I could tell he was fighting the urge to move. I promised myself that, one day, I'd talk him into being a little rougher with my mouth, but for now, I knew he was close. He gasped out a warning, but I didn't pull back.

The salty tang coated my taste buds, and I swallowed every drop, continuing to stroke his shaft until he shuddered, his body telling me it was enough. I sat back on my heels and looked up, wondering if he could understand that I'd meant what I said. That what I'd done had been an apology.

He held out a hand, helped me to my feet, and crushed his mouth against mine. And I knew I'd been forgiven.

Chapter 15

For the most part, the other men aboard the ship ignored me, though they hadn't been happy to see a woman onboard when Gracen had taken me to meet the captain. He'd been pissed too, but Gracen had handed over his father's pocket watch to pay for my passage, and that'd been enough from the captain. Unfortunately, the loss of the watch renewed the friction between us, and I found myself spending most of my time either alone, or in the galley, helping the sailor who was attempting to be a cook.

"Gracen is a lucky man," one of the men said as he took the bowl of stew I made. "To have his woman here with him."

"And a beautiful woman at that," another sailor added in.

"If I had someone like her waiting for me, I don't think I'd be making this run every bloody time," the first man spoke again.

I couldn't suppress my small smile. We'd been on the ship for three weeks, and while I knew names, I hadn't gone out of my way to make friends. I wanted to make as few waves as possible.

More sounds of agreement came from the other sailors, most of which centered around how good my cooking was. I could also hear the quieter comments regarding some other "benefits" of having a wife nearby.

Not that Gracen had been taking advantage of those particular benefits. I forced myself not to look at him during the meal, unsure if I'd be able to handle disappointment or embarrassment, or any negative emotion, in his eyes. The distance hurt, but at least I was with him.

Now I just had to figure out how to be *with* him, or this was going to be the most uncomfortable vacation ever.

The captain had been insistent that Gracen and I take his quarters. Small as they were, they had a bed and, more importantly, a door. A part of me wondered if Gracen had considered declining the offer just so he wouldn't have to be in the same space with me, but I wasn't completely oblivious to the admiring looks I'd been getting from most of the men...including the captain. The fact that Gracen hadn't even hesitated to accept staying with me despite the tension between us told me that he hadn't missed it either.

What none of the crew knew, however, was that even though Gracen and I had been sharing a cabin, we hadn't been sharing a bed. Every night, he waited for hours after I'd turned in, then came into the room and laid down on the floor. I could've confronted him, but I'd taken the initiative once, and I wasn't sure he'd want me to do it again. I knew his relationship with his father had never been great, but Roston was still his father, and that watch hadn't just been about a father and son. It was an heirloom, passed down in the Lightwood family.

And I cost him that.

After almost three weeks, however, I decided I'd waited long enough. I couldn't stand us not being close. In this time and place, I didn't have anyone else. He wasn't just my lover and husband. He was also the only person I could truly be myself with. We were supposed to share our lives, our burdens, and if we were going to do what Washington had sent us to do, then we needed to get our relationship back on track.

The cabin had a single small window placed up high on the wall. While it didn't offer much of a view, on a clear night, it did allow for enough light to see by, so I was able to move from the bed down to the floor without any trouble. Gracen's back was to me, but I knew he was awake.

"Look at me," I murmured. "Gracen, we can't keep going on like this."

For several long seconds, I thought he was going to ignore me, but then he rolled onto his back and looked up at me, his expression unreadable. I brushed hair back from his face, my throat closing up as a wave of love washed over me.

"I miss you." My thumb touched the corner of his mouth, then traced around his lower lip. "Please don't keep pushing me away. I can't stand it."

He reached up and caught my hand. My breath

caught in my throat as he kissed the palm. His other hand curled around the back of my neck, and he pulled me down until our mouths met. Hot, urgent, the kiss was all I needed to know that he still wanted me. There were still things that needed to be said, but for right now, the physical demand was the more pressing matter.

I moved over him, never taking my lips from his. He grasped my hips, grinding me down on him until I shuddered. I shifted, raising up high enough to get my hands between us. When I wrapped my fingers around his erection, he bit my bottom lip hard enough to make my eyes water.

I dug my nails into his chest as I pushed up, balancing myself as I shoved my shift out of the way. I was wet, though not nearly enough for easy penetration. But I hadn't had anything inside me for weeks, and I couldn't wait any longer.

I cursed as I lowered myself onto him, eyes closing, head falling forward. I bit my own lip, latching onto the same tender spot he'd bruised. The sting from my mouth was nothing compared to the pain of stretching too fast, but I didn't even consider slowing down. This wasn't Bruce being in a rush to find his own release, selfishly putting his own needs before mine.

Gracen hadn't said a word, but I could feel the hunger in his touch, in how hard and thick he was inside me. He groaned as I took the last of him into me, a shudder running through my entire body as I adjusted to the intrusion. I couldn't move, could barely breathe. The motion of the ship caused me to rock against him, and the sensation was almost too much.

I opened my eyes to find him watching me, eyes

dark with desire. I began to move, my gaze locked with his. The friction increased my arousal, giving me the lubrication I needed for pleasure to overtake pain. It didn't, however, lessen the intensity of what I was feeling.

His hands were hot as they slid up my legs, moving under my shift to first cup my ass, then one slipping to the front, fingers unerringly finding that most sensitive spot. Once he started to put pressure on it, I knew I wouldn't last long. He sat up, catching me against him, helping me move. Our harsh breathing was loud in the cabin, mingling with the sound of my blood rushing in my ears. I'd pushed myself too fast, too hard, and my climax hit me hard enough to make me cry out, half pleasure, half something else that I couldn't put a name to.

He followed me seconds later, groaning as he emptied himself inside me. We stayed like that, frozen together in the most intimate of embraces, for what felt like a lifetime, then collapsed onto the floor, me with my head against Gracen's heart. My skin tingled as he slowly ran his fingers along the back of my neck, occasionally dipping down below my neckline to follow my spine.

"Did you miss me at all?" I asked the question even though I wasn't sure I wanted to know the answer.

"Of course I did." He sounded surprised that he even had to say it.

"Then why are you keeping me at arm's length?" I propped myself up so I could look at him, shifting so that he slipped out of me. "I'm right here with you. I'm your wife, but I'm also an American, so I know better than anyone what's hanging in the balance here. I don't want to fight anymore, let's just do this together."

Gracen was quiet for a few moments, but it wasn't the tense silence that had permeated our existence recently. It was the thoughtful kind that ensued when he was actually considering my position.

Finally, he spoke, "I swear to you, Honor, the only reason I wanted you to stay behind was because I feared for your safety. I have already lost a wife and the family we might have had. I do not know that I could survive losing you. I used my father's watch and my frustration at you stowing away as excuses to hide from the truth." He brushed his lips across mine. "I won't do it again."

The knot in my chest eased. "There's no guarantee that any of us will be around tomorrow. I've learned that life is too precious to waste on trifles, and I want to spend every moment I possibly can with you, no matter how dangerous it is. I couldn't bear to lose you either."

His arms tightened around me, and I knew that we were okay again. I could put up with anything, I knew, if he was at my side. I could only hope that what lay ahead wouldn't put that to the test.

Less than two days after Gracen and I had patched things up between us, a storm hit. Not one of the little squalls that we'd gone through a few days after we'd sailed, but a full-on storm that made the ship list and tilt dangerously. The sea relentlessly flung heaps of water onto the deck, drenching everything and everyone. After the first day, nothing was dry.

By the second day, I'd been assigned the task of heaving water over the side of the boat with a wooden bucket alongside a slew of other men. The water reentered so rapidly that we hardly made a dent, but I told myself that I was out of my element, and I needed to do what the captain said.

The movement became monotonous, and the world narrowed down to the cold seeping into my bones, the ache in my muscles. It felt as if I'd been tossing water over the side of the boat for ages when the wave of nausea that had been tumbling in my stomach all day hit its peak.

Don't you dare do this now. Hold it together–

I dropped my bucket and dove for the railing. I coughed and sputtered, emptying what little was in my stomach. The wood was slick under my hands, and my feet skidded on the deck. Suddenly, I felt someone grab me from behind before the next pitch of the ship sent me overboard.

I grasped Gracen's shoulders as I turned around. He held me tight, his pale face inches from mine.

"What are you doing out here?! I told you to stay in the cabin."

In spite of the situation, I laughed. "I would've thrown up in there too. The captain said this would help."

Gracen didn't laugh. He pulled us both back, keeping hold of me as a particularly petulant wave rocked the ship hard enough to send us both to our knees.

"Go!" He yelled over the roar of the wind. "It's not safe for you to be out here. Go!"

At any other time, I would have argued, but I was feeling so sick that I did as I was told. I might still throw up, but at least I wouldn't end up in the middle of the ocean while I was puking my guts out.

Not that I had anything left to get out. Each time I felt like I was going to get sick again, all I managed was painful dry heaving. I wanted to sleep it off, but I couldn't bear the thought of trying to sleep while my husband and everyone else was fighting. Still, no matter how much I wanted to help, I knew I had to stay put. So, I screwed my eyes shut, pressing my hand to my unsettled stomach, and tried not to think about anything.

I felt like a failure...and really hoped this wasn't a foreshadowing of things to come.

Chapter 16

It was the beginning of November when we finally reached dry land, and I had a feeling we'd gotten in on one of the last ships. The docks didn't look much different than American ones, but I was still trying to adjust to how much different everything looked from my own time. Not that I'd been to France before, in any time.

It felt strange, the land not moving under my feet, and the lack of movement was almost enough to throw me off balance as I walked down the dock next to Gracen. Most of the sailors had gone on ahead of us, and even though Gracen tried to pretend that they were just eager to get some real food, I knew that most of them were off to find the closest brothel.

I wasn't going to try to explain to my husband how I knew that though. I doubted he'd look kindly on the sort of conversations I'd had with Rogers and Wilkins. Hell, I hadn't even told Bruce half the shit those two talked about.

"We haven't really talked about what we're going to do here," I said.

Gracen nodded. "My family has some

connections over here, but I thought it best if we appear to be on holiday, so we can be a bit more subtle about our inquiries." Something like concern crossed his face. "Washington made it clear that we would be acting in an unofficial capacity, and while our views are not treasonous in France, we will need to be cautious to ensure word of our actions does not reach the wrong ears."

I appreciated the fact that he was including me despite the fact that Washington probably didn't know I'd stowed away, and even more so as I realized that things were still dangerous for us. I hadn't considered what would happen if someone we spoke to ended up reporting what we were doing to someone in England, or even someone back in the colonies. Now, I was even more grateful that I'd come along. If something went wrong, I wanted us to be together.

"Paris is a few hours from here," he continued. "But I thought we would like a day to rest before renting a carriage."

"Good call." I felt like I was staring at everything like an overenthusiastic child. I was so caught up in the novelty of new sights and smells that it took me a moment to think of a question that hadn't occurred to me until now. "How are we going to pay for any of this?"

Gracen looked surprised. "What?"

"You had to trade your watch to pay for my passage. How are we supposed to afford a carriage? A place to stay? Paris?"

He chuckled. "The watch wasn't for your passage, my love." He put his arm around my waist. "That was a bribe for his cabin."

I stopped and stared up at my husband. "I

thought he offered it to us because I was a woman."

"You were a stowaway," Gracen corrected. "And the captain would have been within his rights to throw you in the brig. Which I would have needed to protest. Vehemently."

"I'm confused," I said. "Didn't he know who your father is?"

"He did. But he also knew that my dad isn't fond of you, so I gave him the watch to offer his cabin, and he agreed to use it to retrieve an additional payment from my father for your passage and the use of his cabin."

"An *additional* payment?"

When he grinned, I could see that he wasn't just amused. He was pleased with himself.

"I might have taken my father's seal," he said. "So if I write a letter to promise money, and I use the seal..."

"Your father will have to pay or risk losing face."

"Exactly."

"Damn," I said with a smile. "I married a brilliant man."

His kiss took my breath away, and I almost forgot that we were in public during a time when these sorts of displays of affection warranted attention. When he released me, my face was flushed, hot despite the blustery November weather.

"I cannot wait to get you in a proper bed," he murmured.

I seconded that sentiment, and the two of us moved along a little faster, the tension between us humming as we searched for a place to rent a room. The French proprietress led us to a room on the upper floor, her expression stuck in the chilled mask she'd worn since the moment Gracen had introduced me as his wife.

We'd barely been in the room more than a few seconds before a plain young woman came in with a pail of water. As soon as she emptied it into a ceramic basin, I crossed over to it, already anticipating the cool, crisp feeling. I exhaled appreciatively as I washed my face of the salt water that had soaked into my pores. The soap smelled spectacular, but I was pretty sure that anything would've smelled great after having been packed onto a ship for a month with a dozen men who probably hadn't bathed in a year.

Still, fresh soap and water had always been a part of my coming home ritual, and it helped me feel better now.

I straightened and gave a sigh of appreciation. Gracen wrapped his arms around me from behind, touching his cheek to my damp one, earning another sigh from me, though this one was much more sensual.

"Alone at last," he said, close to my ear. "Truly alone. Did you ever think it would happen?"

I chuckled softly. "I had my doubts. I mean, the cabin was a little more private, but knowing those guys were out there all the time, yeah, it didn't exactly scream *alone*."

"Do you know what I think is an ideal situation?" Gracen asked.

"Hmm?" I murmured.

He pulled me even closer against him. "Having you as close to me as possible, for as long as possible."

"I agree," I answered. "Aren't you glad I snuck aboard?"

Gracen captured my gaze in the mirror, the heat

in his eyes making the answer obvious.

My own body responded with a similar heat. "So, now that I'm here, what can I do to help?"

Gracen lowered his eyes in thought, his hand circling over my stomach.

"I have a question," I asked before he could completely cloud my thinking. "While we're playing Loyalists for the public, am I going to be your servant–"

"You're always my wife," he cut in as he pressed his lips against the curve of my neck.

I turned, lightly scratching his back with my nails. "Am I, you Loyalist snob?"

His embrace tightened. "Remember, you're one too. For now."

I wrinkled my nose in disgust.

He laughed. "You are the one who wanted to come and help in France."

"Mostly I just wanted to be with you," I whispered before kissing him. "I already know how it's going to end. But, I'll do whatever you tell me to."

He raised an eyebrow. "Oh, *now* you'll do what I tell you?"

"Yes. As long as it's pretty close to what I want to do."

He laughed as he released me. We had a few more things to put away, and then dinner to eat. While both of us wanted to take advantage of our room, I had a feeling that after we ate, we were going to take advantage of our bed in a different way. As much as I was looking forward to being able to take our time making love to each other, I couldn't deny that sleeping in a bed that wasn't rocking back and forth was immensely appealing.

I brushed my lips across his, then moved my mouth across his cheeks and chin, making my way toward his neck. I wanted to wake him up in a special way, let him know how thankful I was to be here, with him. The moan escaping from his lips conveyed my success so far.

"How are we doing this morning, my love?" I murmured in his ear as I nipped it and moved back towards his lips. I'd never been one for terms of endearment, but I loved when he called me *my love*.

"What are you doing?"

His question was one of sleepy curiosity rather than lack of interest, so I kept going as I answered, speaking between kisses. "Showing you how happy I am to be able to spend some time with you without worrying about being sea-sick or if one of the crew is going to come knocking."

He ran his hand over my hair, and I lifted my head. My eyes moved to his, and we stared at each other for a moment in complete silence before each moving forward, intent clear, but unspoken, between us. Our mouths crashed together, igniting the fire that always seemed to exist between us, smoldering, waiting for something to ignite it.

My hand fisted in his hair, while he gripped my waist as if I was his lifeline. As his tongue plundered my mouth, my free hand explored the ridges and planes of his torso. The hand on my waist slid up to cup my breast through my shift, and I moaned, back arching as his thumb grazed my nipple.

He broke away just long enough to mutter a single word, "Off," and then began to kiss and bite his way down my neck, mixing the sting of pain with the soft, wet pleasure of lips and tongue. His hands tugged at my shift, and I let him pull it over my head, immediately moving to return the favor.

"You're so beautiful," I murmured as I pressed my mouth against his chest, feeling the heavy thud of his heart. He swore as I circled his nipple with my tongue, his body jerking when I switched to teeth.

Suddenly, he was flipping us over so that I was on my back, staring up at him. His eyes burned into mine as he wrapped his hands around my wrists and pulled my arms above my head. My already racing pulse did a funny little skipping thing, and my breath caught in my throat.

"I have been imagining this moment for far too long," he said as he shifted, moving both of my wrists to one hand so he had the other free. "All I wanted to do the moment you revealed yourself to me on the ship was taste every inch of you."

His hand skimmed over my stomach, dropped between my legs. I parted them eagerly, wanting him to touch me, but he went to my thighs, leaving me frustrated and wanting.

"I sometimes find myself wondering if you are real," he continued to speak, but I wondered if he was talking to himself now. "If I am not touching you, not inside you, then it could be my mind playing tricks on me, torturing me with the idea of loving someone as much as I love you."

His grip on my wrist tightened, his free hand moving up to palm first one breast, then the other.

"The night we were apart, I was unable to sleep, terrified that you would return to your time while I was away, that all I would ever have again was the memory of you." He leaned down and took my nipple between his lips, sucking on it hard enough to make me whimper and writhe.

"I'm not going anywhere," I said breathlessly. In the back of my mind, I knew it was an empty promise because whatever had brought me here could take me back again, and there'd be nothing I could do to stop it, but as long as I had a choice, I would stay.

He moved over me, releasing my hands as he settled between my legs, the tip of him brushing against my curls. He held himself on his elbows, his body resting on mine, but not crushing me. Every breath I took made my already sensitive nipples rub against the hair on his chest, sending shivery sensations across my nerves.

"Love me," I said as I ran my hands down his back to his hips. "Make love to me, Gracen. Remind us both that we are real, that we are here, together."

He took my mouth as he slid inside me, filling me in one slow, sweet stroke. We moved together with a different sort of urgency than the kind that had filled our time recently. This wasn't a race toward release, but a steady building of something significant between us.

The first time I came, it was with a shudder and a cry that he swallowed, his tongue continuing its gentle exploration. I wrapped my legs around him, heels resting just under his ass, and used the leverage to meet him again and again. When I knew he was close, I pulled my mouth away from his.

"I love you, Gracen Lightwood," I said the words with as much force as I could muster. "More than anything, I love you."

He called out my name as he buried himself deep, losing himself in me. I clung to him, his orgasm triggering my own, and we rode it out together.

Together. How we were meant to be, and what I would go to hell and back to keep.

Chapter 17

I was prepared to call myself the wife of a Loyalist, but I wasn't prepared for what it meant to be the wife of a well-to-do man with all the types of connections necessary to help our cause in eighteenth-century Paris.

One of the things I'd never considered about going to Europe two hundred years before I was born was how much of it would actually be the same. There was a joke that said five hundred miles was a long distance to an Englishman, and five hundred years was a long time for an American, and I was seeing that now firsthand.

Buildings that were historical sites recognizable through entertainment were new and fresh. Areas of the city that would become known for their contributions to the artistic community were just starting to come together.

If we'd been here for any other reason, I might've been eager to explore, to enjoy my time. Except this wasn't a vacation. We'd met up with some acquaintances of Gracen's late mother and were staying with them in their new house in the Faubourg Saint-Germain area of the city. Well, *house* didn't exactly convey the sheer size of the place. It was a mansion. An absolutely beautiful, massive mansion.

And after two weeks, I was going stir-crazy.

I'd taken a couple years of Spanish in high school and had picked up a couple words in various Middle Eastern dialects while on tour, but none of that helped me here. The family we were staying with only knew a couple words of English, so they usually talked in French to each other and to Gracen, which left me smiling like an idiot most of the time.

It also meant that it was Gracen who was making all of the initial connections. I'd be on his arm whenever appropriate, but it hadn't taken me long to figure out that my presence here was entirely unnecessary. He didn't need me.

Still, I had to keep up appearances. After all, a big part of this job was being able to blend in, which to the rich meant attending parties and being as superficial as possible. Which meant that if only the men were going out, I had to smile and stay home.

So when Gracen left every evening, dressed in newly tailored clothes, and didn't come back until the early hours of the night, it made me wonder if it would've been better if I'd stayed in Boston. Since we'd left the little inn near the docks, we'd hardly spent any time together, and none of it had been of the intimate nature.

I'd never experienced the feeling of being the little wife who had to stay at home while her husband went out to do all the exciting work. I didn't like it. And I missed my husband.

"You're coming with me tomorrow."

Gracen's words startled me. I hadn't heard him come in, but I wasn't sure if that was because he'd been extra quiet or because I'd gotten used to the small sounds of servants moving around and had subconsciously dismissed his footsteps. I set down the book I was reading – one of the only English books I'd seen – and turned toward him as he came into the room we shared.

I frowned at him, not wanting to hope that I was finally going to get to do some good. "What do you mean I'm going with you? To do what exactly?"

"Remember when you said that the French government wouldn't officially be helping the colonies for a while?"

I nodded. "And they still don't actually support the revolution itself. There were – are – some idealists like Lafayette who want things here to change, but most of Europe is terrified of what will happen if the colonies win."

Gracen sat down on a nearby chair and began removing his shoes. "Then what makes France send assistance at all?"

"From what I remember from my brother, France pretty much just wants to piss off the English, and helping the colonies is the best way to do it." I pulled aside the covers as he finished undressing. "Franklin and Lafayette will be the ones ultimately credited with obtaining France's help, but there were a couple other people who assisted."

"Which is why you suggested that the best way to help was to collect names of sympathizers."

I nodded. "Names and promoting the cause are two of the biggest things we can do."

"Which is why I now need your assistance."

"What can I do? I don't even speak the language." I hoped I didn't sound as whiney to him as I did to myself.

"I have been invited to a ball being thrown by an important man here. Alexandre St. James is extremely influential both politically and socially. Our hosts were able to introduce me, and I was invited to a ball he is holding three nights from now. I believe he may be amenable to supporting the revolution...but he is also a distant relative to the king."

I nodded, understanding his concern though I didn't yet know what good I'd be. "If you say the wrong thing and it gets back to the king, people at court may have connections to British."

"That is what makes this both important and dangerous."

"Does that mean I'm a distraction so you can make a pitch without the wrong person overhearing?"

"No, not a distraction...not exactly. More like a distraction with ears." He leaned back to brush the back of his knuckles down my cheek. "Did you not say that you would be charmingly unsuspicious as a spy?"

I had, though I'd been thinking more about being behind enemy lines back in the States where I'd at least know the names of important players, as well as the important dates. Here, I wasn't sure of much.

"You don't believe that what we're doing here is important," Gracen said suddenly.

"That's..." I sighed. "I just know that our being here won't do any good. Not for a while, anyway."

He gave me a disappointed look. "Have you ever wondered if we have the chance to expedite the process?"

I stared at him. "You mean rewrite history?"

"It is history to you, but the future for both of us. Can you not see the good we could do if we could provide the Continental Army with more support earlier in the conflict? How many lives we could save?"

Shit. I hadn't even thought of that. But now that I was, I was pretty sure it wasn't a good idea. Sure, most people would think it'd be a great idea to make things *better*, but I'd seen and read enough time travel stories to know that the ripple effect wasn't always a good one. For all I knew, if the French helped the colonies earlier in the war, it could change the way the people saw George Washington, and he might not become the first President. America as I knew it wasn't perfect, but I couldn't say that if major changes were made, things wouldn't be worse. Hell, for all I knew, if the Revolutionary War ended one month earlier than it had originally, it could lead to the British attacking at a later point and America losing everything.

But looking at the earnest expression on Gracen's face, I couldn't bring myself to try to explain any of that to him. It was history to me, and a part of my brain had been still seeing it that way. Seeing the soldiers that way. As history.

As dead men.

I forced a smile and ignored the question. "I guess that means I need to go shopping."

Chapter 18

I remembered Bruce joking once that the only worthwhile reason to dance was to avoid any real foreplay. Considering how often he'd used his grinding on me as an excuse to fuck without worrying about me, it wasn't surprising that I hadn't been a fan of going clubbing with him.

As I thought about it, however, I realized any experience of my past life was no help here. Not even dancing.

And as much as I'd kept my cool around some crazy situations, this one was stretching my nerves to the breaking point. The worst part was that I knew my concerns were legitimate. There were too many unknowns here, too many people who could be players in changing history if they had the wrong information.

Then there was the less noble fear. The one that came from not wanting to make a fool out of myself in front of a bunch of French aristocrats.

As I slowly dressed for the evening, I couldn't help but think that it seemed far easier to brave a war zone than go to a French ball. Even though being a medic hadn't put me on the very frontline, it'd been dangerous enough.

My stomach was in knots, my thoughts racing, and I was fairly certain that if I'd eaten anything today, I would've thrown it up already.

I exhaled and smoothed down my dress. I'd needed one of the servants to help me get into this thing, and I could barely manage a full breath. The stays poked my ribs, and the corset shoved my breasts up to create more cleavage than I'd ever had. French styles weren't even close to as modest as the American ones. Hem length, however, was the same, which meant that walking was a pain in the ass. I'd never been the sort of woman who wore skirts short enough to show off my ass, but half a dozen layers that brushed the ground was a bit much.

I couldn't deny I loved the color though. A dark, dove gray that made my eyes look even more silver than normal. A part of me wondered what I would've looked like in a slinky dress made of this same color silk. I had to admit, the thought that I'd never get to wear something sexy, something that I knew would really turn Gracen's head, it bothered me more than I thought it could.

A wave of homesickness washed over me and tears pricked at my eyelids. I'd spent plenty of time away from my family, in strange places, but I'd always known home was there to go back to. I hadn't grown up with a big family, but I had my parents, my brother. They'd always been there for me...and now they weren't even born yet.

"About ready?"

Gracen's voice pulled me away from my maudlin thoughts. They were still there but pushed to the back as I focused on what we had to do tonight. It was too important to go into half-assed.

I turned toward him, smiling as I saw his face

light up. At least he seemed to like my dress.

"You are lovely, my dear," he said as he came over to where I was standing. He pressed his lips to my cheek, lingering to brush his nose against my hair. "If what we were doing was not important, I would keep you here with me all night."

A shiver ran through me, chasing away the last of my ghosts, reminding me why I'd given up one home for another. And that's what Gracen was. My home.

I took his hand, and the two of us descended the stairs. Our hosts had gone on ahead of us, or so I assumed. Sometimes, I felt like they were intentionally avoiding me. That thought did nothing to ease my nerves as Gracen helped me into the carriage. We rode in silence, but his thumb continued to make slow back and forth movements across my knuckles, and I wondered if he was as nervous as I was.

"Take the opportunity to speak to anyone you can," he whispered in my ear as we headed into the St. James mansion. "Listen closely, but be careful what you say."

I nodded in acknowledgment even though he hadn't told me anything I didn't already know. My eyes were wide as I took in our surroundings. I thought the Lightwood estate was beautiful, their parties impressive. But all of that was nothing compared to this. White marble columns, crystal chandeliers, and oak tables loaded with more food than the Continental Army would eat all winter. All of the guests were dressed to the nines, looking fabulous and knowing it full well. They were shamelessly flaunting it as if being just that was inherently theirs and no one else's. The level of snootiness in the air was palpable.

This, I knew, was one of the reasons why the French would have a revolution of their own not long after the American one. For them, it wasn't about taxation without representation or being forced to house soldiers as much as it was the huge gap between the rich and the poor.

"Seen, not heard, at least not with anything of importance. Got it," I muttered back.

He gave me a look that harbored doubt.

Don't worry, I thought. *I won't make you regret me coming along. I'll act like a fine lady, be the perfect socialite wife. I could do this.*

Except, it was obvious the moment we entered the space that Gracen had this all under control. And why wouldn't he? He'd been rubbing elbows with these people almost every night since we arrived. He led me straight toward a tall man with graying sideburns, whose angular face would have been greatly softened by the presence of facial hair. He looked like the type who didn't know how to look at anyone except down the end of his nose.

Lovely.

"Good evening, Giles," Gracen greeted the man with a cordial smile.

The man offered a formal bow in greeting before shaking Gracen's hand. "Gracen."

"This is my wife, Honor." Gracen's hand flexed on the small of my back. "Honor, may I present Giles Moreau."

Giles bowed to me, his beady eyes roving over me in a way that clearly said what he thought of me.

And it wasn't much.

"A pleasure, Madame Lightwood."

"Likewise." My smile felt fake, but Moreau

didn't seem to notice.

"Where is our host?" Gracen asked. "Greeting guests, I presume, but I didn't see him at the door."

"Alexandre keeps as far from the front doors as possible." Giles lowered his voice, his accent thickening. "After an incident involving an angry peasant last month, he prefers to fulfill his duties where he's safely out of reach from the outsiders. It is all this news coming from the colonies. Damn rebels."

Gracen made a non-committal noise and glanced at me. I kept my fake smile on my face and hoped I was playing it right.

Then Giles shocked the hell out of me by leaning closer to us and speaking again. "I would speak with St. James earlier rather than later if I were you. He has a few of his close friends with him, and though I believe they will wait until after they can retreat for cigars and brandy to begin talking politics, it would be best to make yourself a part of their party as soon as possible so it does not appear you are only there for a single purpose."

Gracen glanced around the room, the movement easy, familiar. I'd seen him do it before, at the Lightwood parties, looking for people while trying to not look like he was looking for them. "Where are the others?"

"Durand is in the far right corner. Peitit is by the balcony doors, making eyes at every wife but his."

"And they are all amenable to the suggestions you passed along?"

Giles nodded. "They are. Alexandre, however, remains yours to convince. He is a good man but a stubborn one."

Gracen glanced at me in his peripheral vision,

and I could tell he was checking to make sure all of this had registered. I answered by taking his arm, silently telling him not to worry about me. I would do my part. After all, I had plenty of experience dealing with stubborn men.

I let myself fall into the role I'd accepted as the two of us walked around, smiling and nodding my head as if I could understand a single word they were saying. Well, technically I could understand more than a single word. I knew *bonjour* and *merci*. That didn't exactly help me figure out what my part in all of this was though.

"We are delighted you could join us tonight, Madame Lightwood."

My head jerked around when I heard someone speaking English. Gracen paused, squeezing my arm to ask the question I knew he was thinking. I nodded without looking at him, and he moved on to the next group of men as I smiled at the man who'd addressed me.

"Thank you." I held out a hand.

He took it and kissed my knuckles, bowing over my hand. "Roche Leroy at your service."

"Pleased to meet you." I hoped his English went beyond a few phrases because this was going to be a very short conversation if it didn't. "Are you a close friend of Monsieur St. James?"

"Close?" He seemed puzzled by the term.

I gave him what I hoped was a coy smile. "A confidant. Someone he can trust with his...opinions on certain matters."

Roche's eyes narrowed, but his expression was more one of cautious interest than annoyance. "We do speak on such matters from time to time."

"I'm an American, clearly." I let out a laugh that

was enough like a giggle to make me mentally cringe. "So, of course I'm curious about what people think about this little *skirmish*."

"*Chére madame*, surely you know that France has chosen to remain...neutral at this time."

"Yes, yes." I lightly touched his arm. "But I know that citizens do not always hold the same opinions as their government. Hasn't the Marquis de Lafayette already offered assistance to the colonists?"

"That is true," he said slowly. "But the marquis is young and can afford to be impulsive. After all, one must always be careful what one says, for a nation's loyalties may change." He offered a small smile. "Though I cannot see my country siding with the damn English."

I smiled and gave my best wide-eyed, sweet expression. "Have you spoken to my husband?"

"Not on matters of state or politics," he said, his eyes flicking up to quickly scan the room. "I have spoken briefly with Petit and Moreau, however, and know that we share common opinions."

"Wonderful. Perhaps you could share those thoughts with me so I can pass them along to my husband."

"A woman interested in politics?" His mouth twisted up in mock surprise. "Surely not."

"Perhaps you don't think a woman can be trusted as the holder of such information?" I countered.

Leroy's gaze was appreciative. "By no means. You appear to be quite a capable woman."

I leaned into him, batting my eyelashes and feeling like an idiot. "Does that mean you have a message for me to relay to my husband?"

"And what if I wish to give a message only for you, *ma chére*?" He lightly touched my jaw.

Men. I swallowed a sigh of annoyance and reminded myself of my mission. "You flatter me, Monsieur Leroy." I uttered another giggle that made me want to kick myself. "I'm afraid, though, that what is happening in my home country is foremost on my mind tonight."

"Of course, *ma petite*." He ran his fingers up my arm. "You cannot blame a man for being enchanted by such beauty."

I barely managed to refrain from rolling my eyes.

"Ah," he sighed, "I suppose I must restrict myself to being a political pawn."

That brought a genuine laugh from me. "If I offered to reserve a dance for you, would that soothe your wounds?"

His smile was nothing short of lascivious, but I was quickly getting the impression that was the way French men were in general. "It would, *ma chére*." He started to lean closer, then straightened with a smile that literally went over my head. "Monsieur Lightwood."

I turned to see Gracen coming toward us, his eyes fixed on Roche, a tight smile on his face. "*Ma femme n'est-elle pas belle, mon ami?*"

"*Qu'elle est.*"

The look Roche gave me made me wonder exactly what Gracen had said. I thought I heard the word *belle*, which I knew meant *beauty* or *beautiful*, but that didn't necessarily bring clarity to the conversation.

"Alexandre would like to meet my wife." Gracen took my elbow as he stressed the last two words. "If you will excuse us."

Roche gave us a slight nod that I barely managed to return before Gracen was pulling me away.

"It's not very nice to use another language when you know someone doesn't speak it," I teased.

He didn't even crack a smile. "I assume it is also not nice to flirt with a man who is not your wife."

I stared at him. "You think I was flirting with him?"

Gracen didn't look at me as he stopped us in front of a short, rotund man with a jovial expression and platinum blond hair. "Alexandre St. James, may I present my wife, Honor Lightwood."

"Monsieur St. James, it is a pleasure." I held out my hand. "I have heard wonderful things about you."

"You are a fortunate man, Monsieur Lightwood." Alexandre's dark blue eyes sparkled as he kissed my hand. "And I do not believe I am the only man here who thinks that way."

"As I have seen," Gracen muttered, low enough that no one else heard him.

I, however, could hear the edge to his words, and I didn't like it. I didn't, however, choose to say anything at that moment. Whatever issues my husband and I needed to discuss, we could do it in the relative privacy of our room. Our work tonight was too important to jeopardize.

"You are too kind," I said with a smile. When Gracen shifted next to me, I couldn't help but add, "I have found all the men of France to be equally as kind."

Gracen made a sound that I knew meant he didn't agree with my sentiment – or that he agreed all too much. Before he could add something, a swirl of crimson silk swept into the conversation.

"Ah, Monsieur Lightwood, I would like you to meet my daughter, Alize."

I saw her all at once, as every man there must have seen her. Half a foot shorter than me, she had the sort of curves that I could tell would've been just as shapely without a corset. She had her father's platinum-colored hair, lighter eyes that were a startling royal blue, and fine, delicate features. She was younger than me, eighteen or nineteen, but the wicked sparkle in her eyes made me think the older rather than the younger age.

"Monsieur Lightwood." She gave a little curtsy, her head dipping even as her eyes cut up beneath her lashes. "It is a pleasure for you to join us."

Her accent was thicker than her father's, her voice low and husky. I imagined it was the sort of voice men longed to hear calling their name, accent or not.

"*Le plaisir est pour moi.*" Gracen took her hand and bent over it, kissing the back of it.

Part of me wondered if he was speaking French to piss me off, and then I felt petty for even thinking it.

"Hello," I said, taking a step closer to my husband. "My name is Honor Lightwood. I'm Gracen's wife."

Alize smiled at me, but she kept looking at Gracen, something gleaming in her eyes. I didn't quite recognize it, but I knew I didn't like it.

"Shall we dance, Miss St. James?" He squeezed her hand. "I am certain my wife will be able to entertain your father."

I stared at him, mouth hanging open, as he

swept the cute little blonde out onto the dance floor.

Son. Of. A. Bitch.

The ride back to the house was quiet but teeming with tension...and not the good kind. We stayed at the party for another two hours after our first introduction to Alexandre and his daughter. Part of that time, Gracen had spent dancing with Alize while I chatted up Alexandre and his friends. We hadn't really talked about the real political issues, but men had wanted to know about my life in the colonies, which had made me start to question the wisdom of Gracen leaving me to talk to the men while he danced. Still, I'd managed to tell most of the truth, using what I knew of what the country would become to make a point.

By the time Alize and Gracen had returned, flushing and laughing, the men had seemed to be seeing things my way. They'd also been telling Gracen how lucky he was to have me. Now, however, I had a feeling he wished he'd sent me back to America. After all, if he'd been alone here, he could've used Alize to get closer to her father. I had no doubt he'd have had fun doing it.

The moment we entered our room, he turned on me, eyes blazing, expression furious.

"What were you doing?"

"Me?" I closed the door behind me loud enough for the sound to echo. "I was talking to the guys you left me with so you could go dance with that...*child*."

"She is nineteen. Hardly a child."

"Not the fucking point," I muttered. I started to yank at the ties and ribbons holding my dress up.

"Then what is the point, Honor?" He threw up his hands. "Because I do not understand what you want from me."

I snorted a laugh, liking how unladylike it sounded. "I was under the crazy impression that what I wanted was a husband. Love, cherish, sickness, and health. Everything laid out there nice and simple."

"Did those vows include flirting with every man who paid you a compliment?"

I half-shrugged and shot back, "I know they sure as hell didn't include getting friendly with some teenager."

He frowned. "What is a teenager?"

Right. That was a fairly modern concept. I closed my eyes. "Why do I even bother?"

Suddenly, hands were on my arms, fingers digging into my flesh. My eyes flew open to find Gracen staring down at me.

"Were you jealous?" he asked. "Seeing me dancing with Alize St. James?"

"Yes!" I spit the word out. "I was jealous. I didn't like the way she looked at you, and I hated seeing you with her. Dancing with her. Talking with her."

His mouth twisted slightly into a dark sort of smile. "Good. Because I hated seeing you with those men. You are *my* wife, and I will damn the entire world to hell if it means I get to keep you."

I had a moment to feel surprise before his mouth was on mine, hands moving down to clutch at my waist. There was something different about his kiss, his touch, something that made my insides twist.

"You are mine, Honor Lightwood." He punctuated the statement with a bite at my jaw. "I do not care if it is not fashionable in your time to say such things. You are *mine*."

It wasn't only words. I could feel it in his touch as he pushed me against the wall, as he rocked his hips against me. I dug his fingers into his hair, pulling him back so we could see each other.

"You're mine too, Gracen Lightwood." My voice was breathless, but I made my words as firm as possible. "And don't you forget it."

He pushed at my skirts, his hands finding my ass, gripping it, lifting me. I wrapped my legs around his waist, trusting him to hold me up even as my fingers scrabbled against the heavy wooden door, seeking for any sort of purchase. I felt his knuckles brush against my thigh as one hand moved between us, the other supporting me at the small of my back.

"I need to be inside you."

I nodded, my own yearning as intense as his. I cried out as he drove into me with one hard thrust. His mouth covered mine, swallowing every whimper and curse that escaped as he pounded into me, each stroke more brutal than the last. We'd had no foreplay, nothing to prepare me, and every thrust was a delicious mixture of pain and pleasure, setting off a spark that rapidly turned into an inferno.

My entire body stiffened as I came, and I bit down on his bottom lip. He grunted, hips jerking against mine. I tasted the tang of blood, felt him release inside me, each sensation only adding new heights to what I was feeling. He leaned against me, mouth against my ear, bodies still joined.

"You belong to me, my love. Always."

Chapter 19

News was slow. Like rip my hair out slow, and that was saying something considering that I'd been in the service. When overseas, letters could take forever to arrive. Or, at least, it had seemed like forever...until now. I'd never really thought about how much longer it would take to receive mail when it had to be carried by horse or on foot, then by ship, then again by horse or man. The twenty-first century was all about instant gratification, and what we called "snail mail" was already on its way out – if it wasn't already obsolete. Here, the telegraph hadn't even been invented yet.

The days dragged on, one blurring into the next as I alternated between wandering around the mansion, bored out of my mind, and accompanying Gracen to various functions...pretending not to be bored there. He and I had come to an unspoken agreement where we would occasionally play nice with the locals, but always made sure that it was clear that we were both off limits for anything more than casual flirtations. It curbed the jealousy and kept things from getting too tense between us.

It didn't, however, stop either of us from wondering if we were doing any good here, or if we were just spinning our wheels.

November had just passed its midway point when I found myself in the library, trying to find a book written in English, and a commotion outside caught my attention. I reached the window in time to see a man jumping off the back of an exhausted-looking horse and running for the door. I doubted it had anything to do with Gracen or me, but needing a break from the monotony, I left the library and headed toward the front of the house.

To my surprise, I found Gracen talking to the stranger. Their faces were tense, and even though they were speaking French, their tones told me that whatever news the man had brought wasn't good.

Gracen glanced at me, his eyes confirming my suspicions. He looked back at the man and thanked him before turning to me. Without a word, he took my arm and led me back the way I'd come. Once in the library, he closed the double doors and pulled me back to the farthest corner.

"Did word get back home?" I practically whispered the question even though we were alone.

Gracen shook his head, but his expression kept me from feeling too relieved. "News from the war."

I frowned, trying to remember if there had been any major battles in the fall of 1775, but I couldn't think of any. Then I remembered that I needed to be thinking back to the previous month, and something came to me. It hadn't been a battle, but it was definitely something that had gotten the attention of Europeans.

"Falmouth."

Gracen nodded. "What do you know of it?"

I thought it was a little strange that he asked me rather than sharing what the courier had said, but I didn't argue. Instead, I tried to recall everything I knew about the event.

"October eighteenth or nineteenth, British captain Henry Mowat sent word to Falmouth, Massachusetts that he was there to...well, to punish the town for their part in the rebellion. I think the phrase my brother said Mowat used was 'execute a just punishment.' He thought they'd been aiding the Continental Army."

I could almost hear Ennis's voice as he talked about it on a family vacation to Portland, Maine – the modern-day city that stood where Falmouth had been. I rubbed my hands on my skirt, my palms tingling as my past, present, and future all tangled together.

"The town asked for mercy," I continued. "Mowat told them that if they all swore allegiance to the king and surrendered all of their weapons, he'd spare them. Rather than agreeing, the people began to move out. The next morning, just as his deadline passed, he ordered his ships to fire on the town. When the destruction didn't satisfy him, he sent his men in to make sure the town burned. Afterwards, Mowat left, leaving virtually everyone homeless and having to fend for themselves in the coming winter. And winter in that part of the country comes early, leaves late, and is brutal even with shelter."

I looked at Gracen now and found his face a blank mask. Annoyance flashed through me. These were his people even more than they were mine. For me, this had already happened, and these people were already dead. For him, these were his countrymen being attacked. I'd expected more of a reaction.

"Is that what the courier said?" I asked.

"It is." He seemed to be speaking carefully, choosing specific words.

"And you don't believe him?"

"I asked him what the English response was to the news," Gracen said. "And they are claiming that it is rebel propaganda."

I scowled. "Does that really surprise you? Why would they admit that one of their officers did something like that? It would only make them look bad."

"Admiral Graves is reported to have ordered the attack," Gracen continued slowly. "And his superior issued a statement that said Graves must have had a good reason for his actions. I cannot say that I disagree."

"A good reason?" I laughed, hearing the bitter edge to the sound and hating it. "Look, I might not be from this time, but I know war. There can be all kinds of reasons for going into it, and some of them can seem pretty good, but going after civilians like that...we're not talking about going through a town to find specific supporters. We're talking about retaliation on innocent people."

Something Ennis told me suddenly came back to mind. "Did the courier say what the French government's response was?"

Gracen shifted, his eyes sliding away from me.

"The foreign secretary had something to say about it, didn't he?" I pressed. I wasn't going to offer it unless Gracen said he hadn't heard, but based on his behavior, I was pretty sure he knew what I was talking about.

"The courier reported that the foreign secretary said he didn't believe it."

I gave him a mild look. "My brother quoted to

me exactly what the French foreign secretary said, and that wasn't it. He said, 'I can hardly believe this absurd as well as barbaric procedure on the part of an enlightened nation.' He called it *barbaric*. Hardly the sort of word one uses for disbelief."

"I believe in the cause," Gracen said. "But I know British officers, and I cannot believe that they would attack unprovoked. You were in the army. How can you believe that someone would behave in such an unseemly manner?"

I blew out a breath. "I can't make a blanket statement about officers because I've known good ones who would turn against their own to protect the innocent from something like that, but I've also known ones who take advantage of their position and wouldn't hesitate to destroy a town just because they felt like it."

Gracen folded his arms over his chest. "I believe that we should give gentlemen the benefit of the doubt."

"Are you kidding me?" I fought to keep my temper in check. "You're really going to pull that upper-class bullshit? I don't care if someone's poor or rich, royalty or the son of a fucking garbage man. Unless you know Mowat personally, then I don't give a damn about what his background or lineage or whatever means."

"Wars are fought with dignity, Honor."

I shook my head. "You can tell you've never actually been in one. It doesn't matter when it's fought, war is ugly. Yes, most soldiers are noble and follow the rules, but there are also some who lie and rape and murder because they want to. And there are causes that are worth fighting for, but it doesn't make the death and maiming and horror of battle any less sickening."

His entire body was stiff. "I do not need to have fought in a war to know what it is like."

"There's knowing it in your head, and then there's having experienced it," I said, softening my tone. "It's not a bad thing not to have gone through it."

He shook his head. "But I cannot understand it."

"No, I'm sorry, but you can't."

He gave me a curt nod. "Then I suppose you shall have to retain your opinion, and I shall retain mine."

I blinked at him. "Are you telling me that you don't believe me?"

He raised an eyebrow, and that was answer enough. Myriad emotions flooded me. Some anger, but mostly betrayal and hurt.

"I need some air."

I hurried out before he could try to stop me, but when I didn't hear him calling after me, I knew he wouldn't have even tried. My eyes burned, blurring my vision as I left the house. The sounds and smells of Paris surrounded me, but all I could register was his disbelief. I made my way down the sidewalk, barely seeing where I was going. I could feel eyes on me as I pushed past people, and as soon as I saw an empty street, I ducked down it, realizing after a few steps that I was actually in an alley. Shadows covered me, and the lack of sun made me acknowledge how cold it was, but I didn't turn back. I couldn't go back right now. I had to sort out what I was feeling and what I was going to do about it.

I wasn't aware that I wasn't alone in the alley until my vision went dark. The last thing I remembered was feeling a sharp blow to the back of my head, the sensation of falling, and then...nothing.

Chapter 20

Why did my head hurt?

And why was it dark?

My eyes were closed. That answered at least one of my questions.

As I forced my eyes open, however, I found that answering one question didn't prevent me from having dozens more the instant I saw my surroundings.

I was still wearing my eighteenth-century dress, but that didn't mean anything. I'd come into the past wearing my twenty-first-century uniform, so I had no reason to think that if the reason I'd lost consciousness was because I was going home that my clothes would tell me anything.

I looked around, and wincing pain shot through my skull. Unless I was mistaken, I now knew what had made me black out. What happened next, however, was yet to be seen.

I was in a dark room.

Again, not helpful.

And my wrists were tied.

Fuck.

Then I realized that even though I couldn't see much, I had other senses. Like the skin beneath the restraints. Which I could now tell weren't zip ties. One point toward me still being in the past. Some of the knot around my heart eased.

The fact that my wrists were tied was another bit of evidence that I hadn't returned to my own time, I realized as my head continued to clear. If someone had tied me up, that meant I'd been knocked out on purpose, and that the same person who'd done it had tied me up too. If I'd somehow gotten knocked out in the past and woken up in my original time, the chances of someone finding me and tying me up were pretty slim.

So I was still in November 1775. In France.

While I was thrilled that I hadn't lost my husband, I knew that meant I was in some serious shit.

I slowly sat up straighter, my head swimming at the motion. I could taste the fear in the back of my throat, and I fought to keep it down. A little bit of fear could be a good thing, keep some adrenaline in my system. Panic, however, was bad. It would keep me from thinking clearly, make me prone to irrational decisions.

Like giving up everything I knew so I could marry a man two hundred years in the past.

I would've laughed at the irony if I hadn't been trying not to freak out.

I forced myself to look around, to analyze my surroundings. I was in what seemed to be some sort of cellar. It was devoid of what would typically be present, so it was difficult to tell, but the darkness and absence of windows gave me the inkling I was underground. I could feel some give under my feet, which made me think the floor was dirt.

And also made me realize that I was tied to a

chair.

I wasn't sure if that was a good thing or a bad thing, but I supposed I'd know more when I figured out who had brought me here. It could've been someone French who didn't like me or Gracen because they thought we were British. Or it could've been someone who'd simply wanted to take advantage of a woman on her own.

Both of those seemed to be a bit coincidental, but both options were better than what I suspected the truth to be. That it had something to do with what Gracen and I were trying to do.

I startled when a door banged open. A man strode down the stairs, his features obscured by shadows. He was a big man. Not tall but still large. He carried a lantern in front of him, but I didn't know if that was because it was night, or just that it was dark down here.

"Good, you're awake."

Those three words were enough to tell me that he was English, his accent thick enough to make me suspect he wasn't a colonist. Which actually made my pulse pick up more than it would've if he had been a Frenchman.

"What do you want?" I asked, my voice steady but not confrontational.

"You are Honor Lightwood, ain't you?"

Not high class British.

I nodded in answer to his question as he set down the lantern on a table that I could now see. I was in a cellar, I confirmed. Jars of food were stacked on the shelves, along with other things I couldn't see well enough to name. I could also see my captor more clearly, and wished I couldn't.

He was only a couple inches taller than me, but

broad, muscular. Shaggy gray hair and weathered skin made me put him in his sixties, but then I factored in the bad health that his rotting teeth hinted at and dropped the age estimate by a decade or so.

"Harry Pasternak, at yer service." He gave me an expectant look.

I raised my eyebrows. What the hell did he want me to say to that?

"Let me talk then." He came close enough for me to smell him, and it wasn't pretty. "You and your husband ain't French. And you ain't English."

"No shit, Sherlock," I muttered.

He looked confused for a moment. "Name's Pasternak, I told ya." He shook his head. "Anyway, your husband's family is English, loyal to the king. Somehow, he don't seem to have gotten that message."

A flash of fear went through me. "I don't know what you're talking about."

"Don't you?" Before he could add anything else, the door at the top of the stairs opened.

We both looked up as a young woman with short strawberry blonde curls and charcoal gray eyes came down the stairs, reluctance clear in her every step. She was about average height, a bit curvier than normal, and a sweet, plain face. A face that currently wore the sort of beaten-down, blank expression that, even in my current predicament, made my heart hurt.

"Quit dawdling about, you lazy cow!" Harry snapped at her. He grabbed her arm, roughly yanking her down the last couple steps. The girl released a small yelp but didn't try to pull away. "Just give her the water and then get yer arse to my bed, Celina. Don't make me have to come find you again. I won't be as nice as I was last night."

When the girl – Celina – stepped closer, I could see bruises on her wrists and around her throat, fresh enough for me to know they'd come from the day before. I ground my teeth.

Fucking bastard.

She held a glass to my lips, her hands trembling enough to spill some water down my chin. I gulped what made it to my mouth, realizing for the first time that I was parched. As soon as I was finished, Harry shoved her in the direction of the stairs. She hurried up them, though I was fairly certain she didn't want to be going to his bed any more than she wanted to be down here with us.

"Now, let's return to our conversation." He ran the back of his hand down my cheek.

"I don't know what you want me to tell you."

He grinned. "You're going to give me the names of all the rebels you know in the colonies. Then we're going to talk about how much money your husband will give me to get you back."

Harry began to walk slowly back and forth in front of me, his muscles straining against his filthy shirt as he moved. He reminded me of one of those intimidating Hell's Angels that wore leather from head to foot and guzzled beer by the gallon. Except he smelled much worse.

"I don't know any rebels," I said, keeping my chin up, gaze straight ahead.

Harry shook his head, his expression one of disappointment. Those black eyes of his, however, were alight with something else entirely. Something with which I was certain I didn't want to become acquainted.

"King George will pay me handsomely for each name I give him."

Harry came closer, and I fought not to gag. I was no stranger to the inability to bathe daily, but the man smelled like he'd never even heard of soap...or plain water, for that matter.

"I don't have names," I insisted.

He regarded me for a few seconds before speaking again. "How much do you think your husband will pay for damaged goods?"

The question was without inflection, almost matter-of-fact, and it chilled me to the bone. The meaning of the phrase *damaged goods* wasn't something that had changed from this time to mine, not in this particular type of situation.

"Gracen knows enough people in high places that if you hurt me, you'll regret it."

Harry didn't even blink as he grabbed my hair and whipped out a knife. Not some little blade, but the sort of knife that reminded me of the kind Americans would eventually call a Bowie knife.

"I think it might be worth it," he said as he pressed the cold metal to my cheek. "I want to hear you scream."

If I hadn't been tied up, I might've been paralyzed with fear. This wasn't an empty threat. I could see it in his eyes. He meant it.

He sawed off a chunk of my hair, then bent down and cut a piece of fabric from my dress. "In a bit, your husband is going to get proof that I have you, and he'll be wondering what all I'm doing to you. You're going to sit here and think about giving me what I want in the morning, or I'll find a way to make you talk."

"Waste all the time you want," I said,

summoning up as much bravado as I could. "I can't give you what I don't have."

I saw him draw back his hand, was aware of it coming toward me, but I couldn't dodge the blow. The backhand caught me across the cheek, snapping my head back, and bringing tears to my eyes.

"Tomorrow morning," he said. "And if you so much as try to escape, I will take you apart one piece at a time until you spill all of your secrets. And then I will make you watch me do the same to your husband."

I glared at him, eyes stinging and pride smarting as I couldn't stop the tears from running down my cheeks.

"Fuck you," I spat.

Probably not the smartest thing I could've said, but I wasn't going to give the bastard the satisfaction of knowing how much his threat scared me. I couldn't say for certain that I'd be able to withstand torture, but I knew I'd give up everything if Gracen was put in harm's way.

"Not tonight." Harry showed off his rotting teeth with a barbaric grin. "I got a sweet little thing already waiting to do that."

My stomach roiled at the thought of what he was going to do to that poor girl, of what he'd already done to her.

"And don't go dreaming of some rescue either. No one can hear you in here, and no one else will come down here. Even if anyone knew you were down here, no one's gonna take a prize from Harry Pasternak."

Several seconds later, he was gone, and I was alone in the dark, wondering if this was how history was going to put itself back on track. I'd disappear from the timeline, never to be heard from again. Gracen would return home, thinking that I'd left for my own time, and his path would return to what it had been before I'd come into his life.

"Please," I whispered into the darkness. "Please, Gracen. I'm still here. Don't give up on me."

I repeated the plea over and over again until I dropped into a light and restless doze, my body's feeble attempt to prepare me for what was to come.

Chapter 21

I'd enlisted in the armed forces as a medic, but that didn't mean I hadn't learned how to fight, shoot, and push my body to the limit. I'd been tested physically and psychologically, but when it came to torture, there was only so much a person could be trained to withstand since actually practicing those sorts of vile acts on US soldiers wasn't allowed.

I doubted it would've done much good anyway.

Celina came to see me first, bringing some cold broth that she fed me herself. She refused to look at me and ignored all attempts at conversation, but that didn't stop me from seeing the pained way she moved or the bruises that covered what little skin wasn't covered.

As I watched her disappear back up the stairs, I felt panic creeping in again. As I'd slid in and out of wakefulness through the night, I tried telling myself that it wasn't as bad as it seemed. That Gracen would arrive before Harry could try anything. That my kidnapper wasn't actually as horrific as he appeared. That he wouldn't do any of the awful things he'd said.

One look at Celina and I knew Harry would do all of it...and more.

When I heard the door open again, I clenched my jaw and promised myself that no matter what he did to me, I wouldn't betray anyone, not the ones I knew of personally, nor the people I knew would make history.

"Good morning," Harry said as he came down the stairs.

The light from his lantern glinted off of something in his other hand, and it didn't take much guesswork for me to realize it was the knife he'd used last night to cut my hair and skirt.

"I like knives."

Well, *that* boded well for me.

He looked down at his knife, running his thumb along the side of the blade. "Some guys like to hit to get information, but I find that something a little...sharper works better."

I really didn't like the sound of that.

"Are you going to tell me what I want to know?" He smiled as he came over to me, knife in hand. "Please, tell me no."

"Why'd you have to make things so complicated?" I asked with a sigh. "You want me to tell you no, but you also want me to give you names, and I can't decide which will piss you off more so I can do just that."

His expression hardened, his eyes flashing with anger. He lunged forward, and I was suddenly staring at the tip of his blade, less than an inch from my eye.

"Maybe I should put that eye out. Help you see things better."

I wanted to pull away, struggle against my restraints, but my gut told me that any sign of fear would only spur him on. He meant what he'd said, that a part of him wanted me to refuse to tell him anything so he could torture me.

"I promise you," I said evenly, "that you will not get anything out of me."

He dragged the tip of his knife down my forearm, tearing through fabric and skin. Hot pain flared and blood spilled, but I kept my lips pressed together, refusing to give him the satisfaction of hearing me cry. I didn't know how long that resolve would last, but I hoped it'd be long enough to piss him off.

By the time he left, my clothes were soaked with blood, and my throat was raw from screaming curses at him. Celina came in then and cleaned me up the best she could. The cuts didn't seem to be too deep, which I supposed was good since I didn't need to worry about bleeding to death, but it didn't make them hurt any less.

"Give him what he wants," she whispered as she removed the tattered remains of my gown. "He will not stop until you do."

I shook my head. "I can't. I won't."

Her eyes flicked to mine for a moment. "You will."

I didn't sleep after she left, though consciousness faded in and out. Part of me thought I could almost hear Gracen calling for me, but every time I tried to reach for him, I snapped back into my prison, only to repeat it all over again.

Then he was there again, forcing me to stand so he could start on my back. He didn't use the knife on my breasts, but the way he kept fondling them told me that he'd get to them when we reached the part of the interrogation that he was really looking forward to. The growing bulge in his pants didn't leave any doubt as to what that would be.

After a couple hours, I finally sagged against my restraints, unable to keep myself upright any longer. I was tired, and I didn't know how much longer I'd be able to stay awake. I wouldn't give in, of that much I was certain. I was in more pain now than I'd ever been, but I wasn't even tempted to give Harry anything. What I was afraid of, however, was that I wouldn't wake up at all and that I'd leave Gracen all alone to face a future that he knew just enough about to fear.

It was the thought of him coming for me that made me hang on, made me fight when I knew it would be so much simpler to give up.

"I think perhaps it is time to abandon this course altogether."

My eyes opened, but I still couldn't get my feet underneath me. Harry leered at me, the expression on his face clearly saying what he had in mind. He grabbed my hair, jerking my head up until we were face to face. His free hand grabbed at my breast, squeezing hard enough to hurt. Or, at least, it would've hurt if almost every other part of my body wasn't already in agony.

"Listen good," he said, tightening his grip on my hair. "You ain't gave me anything, and your husband clearly ain't gonna pay, so I got to get something out of it. And if I do it right, maybe you'll tell me what I want to know."

"Never."

He grinned. "We shall see."

He let go of my breast and shoved his hand under my shift and up between my legs. I tried to twist away, tears running down my face as he tried to get his fingers inside me.

"That the best you got, you fucking son of a bitch!"

He laughed as he shoved me away from him, my arms jerking painfully against my restraints.

"You ain't gettin' off that easy," he said as he straightened. "I aim to take my time with you."

I barely suppressed a shiver, and it wasn't one of anticipation. He grabbed his crotch, rubbing as he licked his lips. For a moment, I wondered if he'd get himself off like that, then leave me for the rest of the day.

"I'll be back."

He disappeared up the stairs, bellowing for Celina as he went. The door slammed, and a few seconds later, I heard a woman's voice. I couldn't make out the words, but the tone was clearly pleading. His voice was louder, accompanied by a few solid thunks that I knew were fists on flesh.

Then she started to scream...

Chapter 22

I pulled my knees up to my chest, pressing my forehead against them, trying to block out everything around me. Though it had been quiet for a while now, Celina's screams were still imprinted in my head, playing over and over and over again. I'd heard screams like that before, ones that were full of as much pain as they were terror, and I knew that she was being tortured. Not like I was, with cuts designed to extricate information, but for Harry's pleasure alone.

When she'd gone quiet, my imagination filled in the blanks with all sorts of horrible what-ifs. Harry could have satiated his appetite, which meant he'd be returning to me, and it would be my turn to scream. He might have simply silenced her, but I doubted it. Everything I'd learned about him told me that he was a sadist – not the kinky S&M kind but the sadist sociopath kind. He'd want to hear her suffer. Which meant that her silence could have come from her passing out. In which case, he was either continuing to abuse her unconscious body or was quickly tiring of torture without any response.

Or he'd killed her.

Based on what I believed he was doing, I wasn't

sure that death was the worst of the options.

Suddenly, footsteps were coming this way, and I knew my time was up.

I tried to ready myself for what was to come even though I knew that no length of time or mental toughening would prepare me for what I knew he was going to do to me. Just as every soldier on active duty knew that capture and torture was a possibility, every female soldier knew that rape was almost certain if she was taken prisoner.

That knowledge still couldn't prepare me for the fear that coursed through my body. It didn't stop me from pulling at my restraints even though I knew I couldn't get free. It didn't keep me from running through a thousand different scenarios as I tried to decide the best way to respond once Harry started putting his hands on me. From a medical perspective, I knew that the more I fought, the worse he would hurt me, and from a psychological standpoint, if my guess about him being a sexual sadist was accurate, then the more I struggled and the more I hurt, the more aroused he'd become.

Despite all of that, I wasn't sure I could voluntarily refrain from resisting. I knew there was the possibility that my body would freeze on its own, that I'd be unable to fight back. But I didn't think I could make it a conscious choice.

The door opened, and the top step creaked. Adrenaline dumped into my veins, racing through my body. The good part of that was that it chased away the pain from my wounds, the bad was that I was completely and totally aware of everything now. Any hope I'd had of blacking out was gone for a while.

I pulled at my restraints, barely able to feel the

ties biting into my wrists. "I don't care what you do to me, I'm not telling you shit." My voice was rough, and it hurt to talk, but I wasn't going to give Harry the satisfaction of knowing how terrified I was. "When I get free, I'm going to kill you. Slowly."

He hadn't brought a lantern with him, and not being able to see him coming made it so much worse. I could hear his breathing, hear the shuffle of feet on dirt, and my entire body tensed, trembled. Tears spilled down my cheeks, and I found it hard to breathe.

I couldn't take it anymore. "Just get it over with, you bastard!"

Suddenly, he was there, and I braced myself for his touch, for the smell of him...except it didn't come.

"Shhh, Honor. I need you to be quiet now."

The familiar voice didn't register at first, my brain rationalizing it as me hearing things. But then I caught the natural scent of sweat and soap.

"Gracen?" I whispered his name, hardly daring to hope.

I heard the sounds of flint and tinder. A flicker of flame and light made me hiss, narrowing my eyes, but then I saw him and something inside me cracked. His hair was tied back, letting me see how drawn and tired his face was. He set down a candle and turned toward me. One of his hands cupped my neck as he fit my whole body perfectly into the curve of his. I sagged against him, a small sob catching in my throat. Pain lanced through me, but I welcomed it because it came with the safety of his embrace.

"You're here. I never thought I'd see you again. I thought..." I let the words trail off as he eased me back onto my feet.

"We need to get you out of here," he said softly.

I flinched as he drew a knife from his belt, and his eyes widened. I watched his gaze sliding down over me, fury filling his face as he fully registered what he was seeing. I could only imagine how I looked, my shift soaked with filth and blood. I was too exhausted to feel any embarrassment, though I was sure it would come later.

"I am going to cut your hands free," he said, his expression back under tight control.

I nodded my understanding, forcing myself to remain still as he came closer with the blade. I reminded myself that Gracen would never hurt me, that I had nothing to fear from him. As soon as I was free, he put the knife away and started to reach for me.

"I do not want to hurt you," he said as he hesitated.

"I can't make it alone," I admitted. "I need to lean on you, at least for a minute or two."

He nodded, sliding his arm around my waist. I gritted my teeth as blood began to flow back into my arms and hands. The wounds throbbed, and I could feel some of them breaking open again as I moved. Gracen didn't say a word as we made our way toward the stairs, but I could feel the tension in his body.

When we reached the top, I stopped short, a thought popping into my head, preventing me from going any farther. "No, no. Wait."

Gracen looked thoroughly confused. "Honor? Wait for what? We need to leave now, before anyone realizes that you are gone."

"Celina. I can't..." I shook my head, wincing as a sharp stab of pain went through my skull. "Have you seen a girl?"

"No." He shifted, tightening his hold on me enough for me to sense his anxiety. "Honor, we must go. *Now*."

"She's a servant here, and he's been hurting her," I said. "We have to find her. I won't leave without her."

Chapter 23

Gracen muttered a few words that had something to do with stubborn women, then spoke to me directly, "We need to leave, my love. You are hurt, and we are in danger the longer we linger here."

"He tortured her, Gracen," I said. "Raped and tortured her. Repeatedly. And that's what he planned on doing to me. I can't leave her to that. If he hasn't killed her already, we have to take her with us."

My husband's eyes met mine, and I knew he could see that I meant what I said. He nodded once, and then we started toward the nearby staircase. Every inch of me screamed in protest as we climbed to the next floor, but I pushed the pain to the back of my mind, focusing instead on how to figure out where Celina was. For all I knew, this house was full of people who'd be all too happy to finish what Harry had started.

As we reached the second floor, however, a pained cry told me that we were in the right place. I pulled myself free from Gracen and went for the first door I saw. Without thinking about the possible consequences, I pushed open the door.

It took me only a few seconds to register the scene, and it was enough to make me want to throw up.

Celina was on her side, facing the door, stripped naked, body bruised badly enough I could see the discoloration through the blood. Sections of skin looked like raw meat, and a couple of her fingers stuck out at such odd angles that I knew bones had been broken. Her charcoal gray eyes were dull and glassy, her entire body shivering from shock.

Harry was behind her, and I didn't need to see details to know what he was doing to her. Just like I knew that this wasn't the first time he'd done it.

Rage burned away everything else inside me, and I was moving before Harry could react. My wounds slowed me enough that Gracen reached Harry before I did, grabbing the startled man by the arm and yanking him off the bed. I went for Celina, trusting Gracen to deal with the sick bastard.

"It's okay," I said as I went to my knees. "We're getting out of here, and you're coming with us."

She blinked slowly, eyes still unfocused. I took her face between my hands as gently as I could. I heard the men scuffling behind me, cursing and hitting, but I kept my eyes on her. I might be able to walk out of here with a little help from Gracen, but she had to be able to do that too. If she had to be carried, I didn't know that we'd all be able to make it, and I'd be damned if I was going to leave her behind.

"Celina, I need you to listen to me. I know you understand at least some of what I'm saying, so I hope you can get enough to understand that I can't carry you. Can you walk?"

A loud thud made me want to look behind me,

but I forced my eyes to stay on Celina.

"You put your hands on my wife." Gracen's voice was low, deadly. "You hurt her. You hurt that girl. Violated her–"

Harry cackled, the sound wild. "Girl's no more than a whore."

My hands curled into fists as I heard a thunk of flesh against flesh, the change in Harry's laughter telling me it'd been Gracen who'd delivered the hit.

"Celina." I pitched my voice low. "Please, you have to listen to me. We have to go."

Her eyes finally slid to mine and held. She nodded, her hands pushing against the mattress as she tried to sit. She gestured toward the ground, and I looked down to see her dress. I handed it to her, but just as her fingers closed around it, she jerked back, eyes wide as she whimpered.

Before I could react, I was yanked back by my hair. A fist collided with the side of my jaw, and new pain exploded. My head spun as I struggled, then, suddenly, the pressure on my scalp vanished. I heard Gracen shouting, but things were starting to go gray.

"Madame?" A shaking hand touched my arm, and I looked over to see Celina kneeling next to me.

Everything rushed back with overly bright clarity, and I scrambled to my feet. In the few seconds I'd lost, everything had gone quiet. I turned, scared of what I'd see.

Harry was sprawled on the floor, dead. Blood still gushed out of his mouth, his eyes wide open, staring at nothing. Gracen knelt over him, chest heaving, knuckles bloodied. I didn't remember making a sound, but I must have because Gracen turned and looked straight at me.

His face went pale, and he stumbled as he came toward me. His arms went around me, pulling me against his chest. I wanted to stay there, to relax into his embrace, take the comfort he could offer, but I knew we couldn't. I didn't know where we were, or if Harry had people who'd be coming after us, but I knew we needed to get out of there.

"We need to go," I said as I pulled back. I nodded toward Celina. "Help her."

The look on his face told me that he didn't want to let me go, but that he also knew Celina was in worse shape than I was. He looked down at her, and she shrank back. I put out a hand, lightly resting it on her shoulder.

"It's okay, Celina. He won't hurt you. We're going to get you out of here, but he needs to help you."

Fear was still written on her face, but she nodded at Gracen, allowing him to sweep her up in his arms. I grabbed onto his arm using him for balance as we made our way back out into the hallway. I kept waiting for someone to come out, to demand to know what we were doing, to threaten us, but we made it all the way to the front door before someone finally noticed us.

"*Vous ne pouvez pas la prendre!*"

I didn't need to speak French to know that the woman shouting at us didn't want us to leave. Gracen paused, the two of us looking over toward the owner of the voice.

"These women have been abused. My wife kidnapped, held against her will. If you wish to contact the authorities regarding your servant, you will need to be prepared to answer for that as well."

The woman had such a look of fake incredulity

that it was obvious she'd known what Harry had been up to, including me.

"I do not know what you mean."

"Bullshit," I snapped. "We're going to leave now, and if you come after us, I'll beat the shit out of you myself." I gave her a nasty smile. "And I really hope you can understand me, you heartless bitch."

Judging by the look she gave me, she understood enough.

The lady dropped the act and started screaming in French, bringing a man running. A man who looked both furious and oddly familiar. He began to yell too, and it was clear from Gracen's clenched jaw and angry gaze that nothing they were saying was complimentary.

"Come with me, Honor," Gracen said, his voice quiet but firm. "They will not try to stop us."

"And if they do?" I muttered.

"Then I will stop *them*."

That was all I needed to hear. No matter what we'd argued about, he was willing to kill for me. He *had* killed for me.

We hurried down the stairs of what I now saw was a boarding house. A carriage sat in the street in front of us, and Gracen took us right to it. He had me get in first, then handed me Celina. As he climbed in after us, he pulled the door shut behind him and hit the front of the carriage. Immediately, it started to move, bumping over the streets at a fair clip. Celina moaned but seemed to be losing consciousness. I put my arms around her, let her lean on me even though all I wanted to do was have Gracen hold me.

He put his hand on mine, squeezing it. "You are safe now. Both of you."

"Where are we going?" I asked.

"A house on the outskirts of the city," he said, his fingers tightening around mine. "Alexandre St. James owns it. Alize offered it as a safe haven."

Alize.

Damn her.

Chapter 24

I was so not ready to watch Alize fawning all over my husband again, but I wasn't so petty that I'd refuse a safe place because of my jealousy, especially when the young woman in my arms was in need of medical attention.

The carriage hit a bump, and I sucked in a breath. I needed some doctoring too. I'd lost enough blood that I was a little light-headed, but I didn't think I was in any real danger. Celina, on the other hand, was a real mess.

I could ask Gracen to fill me in on the blanks later. Right now, we both had more important things to worry about. As the carriage came to a stop, I shifted Celina over to Gracen and watched as he lifted her out. I followed him, trying not to grimace when I saw a familiar blonde running out of the huge house in front of us.

To my surprise, however, she didn't look like the flirty, prissy thing she'd appeared to be at the ball. She looked like she was concerned. Beyond concerned, actually. She looked almost panicked.

"*Par ici! Rapidement! J'ai un docteur qui attend!*"

Gracen followed her, and I followed him, every

step more excruciating than the last. I really hoped I'd understood at least one of the words Alize had said as being *doctor*, because while I had medical training, I could feel myself fading fast, and I wasn't sure I had it in me to be as thorough as I would need to be not to miss anything.

Alize led us up a flight of stairs and into a small room. She rattled something off in French, pointed at the bed, and then hurried off. Gracen set Celina down, and I went toward them. I wasn't sure if there was a doctor coming, so I'd do what I could and hope that it would be enough.

Celina was only half-conscious as I leaned over her, but her eyes managed to stay on me as I spoke to her, my voice low as I explained what I was going to do. I doubted she knew enough English to understand the specifics, but it seemed to keep her calm as I stretched out her arm and looked at her hand.

A man started speaking French behind me, and he didn't sound happy. I flinched as someone touched my shoulder but relaxed almost immediately when I recognized Gracen.

"Let the doctor through, Honor." He eased me up and to the side. "We need to get you taken care of now."

I wanted to protest, but I knew he was right. All of the pain I'd been suppressing was making its way past the endorphins that had flooded my system. The cuts weren't deep, but an infection during this time could be deadly. I asked Gracen for water, soap, and clean bandages as I took a seat on a nearby chair, watching as the doctor started to examine Celina.

Gracen began to help me wash up, his

expression darkening more with each new wound he saw. Behind us, I could hear Alize and the doctor conversing in French, but their voices were low enough that even if I understood the language, I still probably wouldn't have been able to tell what they were saying.

By the time we finished with my hands and arms, they were thrumming with pain and it was all I could do to keep back the tears. I couldn't cry, not here, not now. Maybe later, I'd be able to let go, but for the moment, I had to stay strong.

Suddenly, Gracen stiffened. He whispered his question. "Is bleeding still a medical practice in your time?"

My eyes went wide, and I shook my head. "No. That's a bad idea. Makes a person weak. Can even kill them."

He stood and turned, saying something in French that made the doctor and Alize both look up. The doctor looked annoyed, Alize concerned. A rapid exchange followed, Gracen and the doctor both becoming increasingly annoyed, voices rising until Alize finally shouted at them both.

Gracen said something that included my name, and all eyes turned to me.

"Will you help her?" Alize asked, tears brimming, ready to spill. "Please, Madame Lightwood. Please help her."

It was in that moment that everything clicked into place.

Rather than answering Alize's question, I asked one of my own, "How long have you been in love with her?"

She lifted her chin, her eyes taking on an arrogant light, as if she was daring me to judge her.

"Six months. From the first moment I saw her. She loves me too."

Everything made sense now. This was why she'd been all over Gracen at the ball. She'd been hiding her sexual orientation. In a country founded by Puritans, homosexuality was a taboo that wouldn't be spoken of in public conversation for centuries. No matter how much I wanted to be annoyed at her for having flirted with my husband, now that I knew the reason why, I couldn't be angry.

"I don't doubt she does," I murmured. "I'd be happy to take a look at her."

Alize said something to the doctor that made him scowl, then stomp off in a huff. She looked at me as she sank down on the edge of the bed, as she reached for Celina's hand.

"We need to take off your dress," I said. "I need to see how badly he...hurt you."

Celina's face flushed, and I knew she'd understood what I meant. Then I heard a choking sob and realized that Alize hadn't known how bad things were.

"He...did he...?" Tears spilled down Alize's cheeks. "Oh, *mon chéri.*"

"I'll be as gentle as I can," I promised.

I didn't realize that Gracen had left the three of us alone until I finished my examination and applied cold compresses. She didn't look like she needed stitches, but she had enough tears and cuts that she was going to be healing up for a while. The doctor had already set and bound her hand, so when I was done, the only thing left to do was get her dressed and pray that she didn't get an infection. For that, I'd have no solution. Not in this time and place.

"*Merci*," Celina whispered as Alize helped her

into a loose shift.

"You and Gracen may stay here as long as you like," Alize said, her eyes still focused on the woman she loved. "All I have is yours."

I started to turn, to leave so I could find Gracen, and we could go to bed, but something gave me pause. Maybe it was a result of blood loss or the fact that I knew some of what Celina had suffered had been a result of Harry's torturing me, but I had to say something.

"I knew a man once who didn't want to be with a woman. He was attracted to men. And he was one of the best, bravest men I knew." I met Alize's gaze, then Celina's. "Don't let anyone tell you that who you love makes you a bad person."

Alize reached out and squeezed my hand. "Thank you."

I gave her a tentative smile, starting to go before I paused again. A thought had just struck me. "If you don't mind me asking, how did you know...how did Gracen know to come here?"

"Celina was able to sneak out a message late yesterday afternoon, told me that a woman was being held prisoner. I had spoken to Gracen a few hours before about your disappearance. I hoped that he would find you and bring word of Celina. I had not heard from her in days." Her fingers tightened around my hand. "Thank you for saving her."

I couldn't speak around the lump that had just formed in my throat, so I simply nodded before leaving the two women alone.

Chapter 25

Gracen was waiting outside the room, clearly having left only to give Celina privacy. He knew what Harry had done to her. His eyes locked with mine, but he didn't say anything, merely held out his hand. I took it, letting him pull me after him down the hall and into an empty room.

A bowl of clean water and what smelled like witch hazel sat next to the bed. A maid stood next to it, setting out some rags and towels. As soon as she saw us, she murmured something in French and hurried out.

Without a word, Gracen reached for the bottom of my shift and lifted it over my head. A muscle in his jaw twitched as he tossed the bloody and ruined garment to the floor. He soaked one of the rags in the water and began to clean each wound. I clenched my jaw so tightly that my teeth ached, but I knew I couldn't make a single sound of pain, not without hurting Gracen too.

By the time he was finished, my muscles were weak and trembling, and I needed his help to slip between the sheets. I watched as he pulled off his clothes and wiped himself clean, but I didn't say anything either. I had the vague impression that it was morning, but I didn't plan on leaving this bed anytime soon.

As soon as he climbed into bed next to me, I pressed myself against him, shivering as his arms immediately went around me. He kissed the top of my head, his embrace tight enough to let me know that he'd been almost as scared as I'd been.

"I will never let anyone hurt you again. Do you hear me? Never again."

It took all the strength I possessed, but I lifted my hand to stroke his cheek. He leaned into the touch, then turned his head to kiss my palm. His fingers lightly touched the bruised part of my jaw where Harry had punched me.

"Did he...that man...did he do to you what he did to..."

I knew what he was trying not to ask, and I shook my head. "No. He hurt me, but he didn't..."

Gracen breathed a sigh of relief and rested his forehead against mine. "I thought I had lost you." He ran his hand over my hair, the gesture soothing me in a way that went beyond the aches and pains in my body. As my eyes started to close, I heard him whisper, "Rest now, my love."

Knowing I was safe, I gave in to the exhaustion and let myself fall asleep.

The knife was cold against my throat. His breath was foul, his voice was like death itself,

promising pain and humiliation. Hot blood trickled down my neck as a bright flash of pain lanced across my skin. His words echoed in my ear, each one more graphic and chilling than the last.

I wanted to struggle, to fight back. Even if he overpowered me, I would at least know that I'd tried. Except I couldn't move. Something had me stuck in place, unable to do anything but listen to the horrible things he was saying, the disgusting details of what he'd done to Celina.

What he planned to do to me.

I tried to scream for Gracen, for help from anyone, but I knew help wasn't coming. No one was coming. I was alone.

"Honor."

Another voice, a warm voice, came through the darkness, coaxing me forward.

"Wake up, my love. I am here. Wake up."

I gasped as I jerked awake, struggling for a moment against the arms that held me. I recognized the scent a moment before his voice registered.

"You are safe, darling. I have you," he murmured soft words as he held me, rocking me gently in an attempt to calm me down.

Even as my breathing calmed and my pulse slowed, he shifted us so that I was on my back again, and he was propped up on his elbow. His movements were slow and non-threatening as he slid his hands over my waist, placing a few soft kisses on my cheeks, my lips. I wrapped my arms around him, inviting him closer, needing the comfort his arms offered. He buried his face in the curve of my neck, lips moving against my skin, his gentleness easing the tension inside me.

"I need you," I whispered as I tugged at his shirt.

The room was chilled, the fireplace down to coals, but Gracen's skin was hot, and I craved the warmth.

He pulled his shirt over his head, then reached for mine. I made a pained sound as the movement pulled at my wounds, and Gracen leaned over me, concern replacing the lust in his eyes.

"I'm okay," I said. "I need you."

I tried to pull him down on me, but he shook his head and slid down the bed. My stomach clenched, heat pooling in my belly as he lowered himself to the mattress and pulled my legs over his shoulders. Neither one of us had been virgins before we met, but he'd been strictly missionary position with his previous wife, and my ex-fiancé hadn't been the most attentive lover, so we were still exploring what we liked.

I whimpered as he ran his tongue over me, then cried out when he flicked the tip of my clit. The first time he'd gone down on me, I'd had to instruct him, but he was a quick learner. He used all of that knowledge now, adding new bits as he listened to my responses. He had me writhing in moments, coming less than a minute after that.

And still, he continued to use his mouth on me, coaxing orgasm after orgasm until I was practically sobbing his name. Only then did he slide back up my body, his erection hot and hard against my hip. I shuddered as another aftershock rocked through me. I felt like my skin was buzzing, like every cell had been infused with electricity. Any pain I might've felt was gone, absorbed into the bliss that he'd given me.

"I swear to you, Honor, I will never let anyone hurt you again." He brushed hair back from my face.

I rolled onto my side, hooking my leg over his

hip and pulling him to me. He started to shake his head, but when I wrapped my hand around his cock, he moaned, all of the fight going out of him. He moved forward, joining us together with one smooth stroke. His mouth found mine as we rocked against each other. Our tongues explored, teased, and we took our time with each other, relishing the feel of each other's bodies, the knowledge that we were alive and together.

When I finally came, Gracen's cry mixed with my own, his body stiffening as he followed me over. He pulsed inside me, filling me, reminding me that I was his. The way he clung to me was also a reminder. One that said he was mine as well. We'd deal with things as we had to, but not right now. Now, it was about simply being together.

Chapter 26

Though it was a difficult pill to swallow, the reality was that Gracen and I needed to lay low for a while. While looking for support for the colonies wasn't illegal, murder and theft was, and Gracen had killed a man. It didn't matter that he'd been protecting Celina. We discovered that she'd been an indentured servant which meant Celina was considered enough like property that we could be arrested for removing her from the house, and since her masters had given permission for Harry to do as he wanted with her, he hadn't really been breaking any laws. Not laws anyone would enforce, anyway.

So we needed to stay hidden until we figured out what we were going to do next.

Celina was recovering quickly, physically at least. Her emotional scars...those were going to be harder to mend. With Alize at her side, however, I thought it might go faster than it would have otherwise. I couldn't deny that my respect for the girl had grown over the past couple days. Gone was the flighty, flirty brat she'd pretended to be. She was caring and attentive to everything Celina needed, gracious and grateful to Gracen and me. She was far more mature than I'd ever thought she could be.

Her father had come to visit, but Gracen and I

had made ourselves scarce, giving them the privacy they all deserved. I didn't know how much Alexandre knew about Alize and Celina's relationship, but I didn't see how anyone could see the two of them together and not know they were in love.

My own injuries were healing as well. Since none of my cuts had been deep, as November gave way to December, they turned from wounds into scars, and I found myself believing that they may eventually fade altogether.

What wasn't fading was the feeling that we'd failed, Gracen and I. We'd come to France to find help but ended up making a mess out of things. Or, rather, I had. If I hadn't left the house that day, then Harry wouldn't have grabbed me. None of this would've happened.

Every time I started to think like that, I reminded myself that Harry had been abusing Celina long before I'd come along. If my presence had made him get more violent than usual, it had also led to us rescuing her. Not that it made anything she'd gone through any less horrific.

It was strange, the four of us strangers being bound together by something so awful. Well, two couples who were strangers to each other anyway. Strangers who were stuck together while we waited to decide what to do.

Waiting was boring. It didn't matter if it was being done in a tent in the desert or a house in the past. When the only changes were slight variations in diet, and which maids scurried out of which rooms, boredom was inevitable.

Then, on the second of December, a paper came with the first major news of the war since the burning of Falmouth.

I couldn't read enough French to know what the article said, but the expression on Gracen's face told me that it was important.

"On October twenty-sixth," he summarized, "King George met with Parliament and officially declared that the uprising in the colonies must be dealt with. England has officially acknowledged that they are at war with the colonies."

A moment of silence fell between us, and I knew that he was waiting for me to make some comment about how I'd been right all along, how his doubting me had hurt. How if he hadn't said those things to me, I might not have been out on the street to be taken by Harry.

I didn't say a word. I didn't need to. Not when the proof of everything I'd said was right there in black and white. I turned to look out the window.

He set the paper down and came up behind me. "You have every right to be upset with me. I did not believe in you, and I had no right to doubt. Not after all we have been through."

He reached for me, and though I didn't return his embrace, I didn't resist either. I let him wrap his arms around me, pull him back against my chest. He pressed his lips to the spot behind my ear that made me shiver.

"Forgive me, my love." His words were soft in my ear. "I never should have doubted you, and I never will again. We may argue – I can almost guarantee that we will – but I will not doubt."

I let the air out of my lungs with a sigh and closed my eyes. "Of course I forgive you, Gracen."

"Thank you, sweetheart." He kissed the top of my head. "Now, come with me."

"Where are we going?" I asked as he took my hand and turned me around.

"To bed," he said with a mischievous grin. "I have a lot to make up for, and plenty of time to do it."

Chapter 27

Alexandre returned from a visit to court a week after Gracen and I read the headline that solidified the things I'd said would come to pass. I wasn't entirely sure what the relationship between Monsieur St. James and King Louis XVI was, but I knew it was close enough for Alexandre to have spent time with the king and his advisors. Which meant that when he asked to speak to Gracen and me the day after he'd arrived home, a knot formed in my stomach and stayed there as I quickly dressed.

The best part of us having been essentially housebound for weeks was that I hadn't needed to put on all the under-shit on when I got dressed. I'd been fine with a shift and dress. For this, however, I went all-out. It took me longer than usual to get it done, but when I was finally ready, Gracen was still patiently waiting.

He held out his arm, and I took it, falling into step next to him as we made our way down the hall, down the staircase, and into the front parlor. My fingers were cold in his, and he squeezed them as we went, a gesture I knew was meant to be reassuring. Considering what was on the line, however, I could only be reassured so much.

Alexandre was waiting when we entered, but he

wasn't the only one. To my surprise, Alize and Celina were sitting on the nearby loveseat. They weren't holding hands or anything like that, but they were sitting close enough that their knees were touching. Celina looked nervous, and I didn't blame her. I had no idea how much Alexandre knew about the relationship, or what he thought of what he did know, but he hadn't kicked her out, so that was something.

"Please, sit." He gave us both warm smiles. "We have much to talk about."

Gracen sat in a chair while I perched on the arm next to him. He took my hand, and I could feel the tension in his touch.

"Tell me what progress you have made gathering support for the colonies."

I automatically stiffened but reminded myself that Gracen and I couldn't get in trouble here. Not for this. And Alexandre had been supportive before, so there was no reason for me to be nervous. Especially since he'd let us stay at his home without question.

I only half-listened as Gracen explained the things he and I had gone over half a dozen times in the past couple days. I had all of it memorized, but it was the first time Alexandre had heard most of it.

"England and France do not have the best relationship," St. James said as Gracen finished. "And there are many who are hoping that the English will receive a, how do you say, comeuppance."

"Do you?" I asked.

"I cannot deny a part of me would enjoy that." He smiled, his eyes sparkling. "But, despite my position, I do not believe that the wealthy are entitled to more than the poor."

"Does that mean you are willing to provide support for the colonists?" Gracen asked. "Official financial support?"

"There are many at court who want to see the English lose," Alexandre said. "Both for vengeance and to weaken their power, but there are just as many who fear that if the colonies win their freedom, revolution will spread to France."

I could almost hear my brother's voice, filled with his usual exasperation, as he explained to me the role the American Revolution had had in sparking similar uprisings, including the French Revolution. The loss had not only weakened the British Empire, but had set off a chain reaction that changed the world, showed people that power wasn't always connected by money. There were the rare people in high society who had wanted change, but they'd been exactly that. Rare.

I couldn't, however, come right out and say what all I knew. I needed to be more subtle than that.

"I understand the need to be cautious." I chose my words with care. "But can we really blame people for wanting equal treatment? For their voices to be recognized?"

Gracen squeezed my hand, and I felt his unspoken warning to tread carefully. There was a huge difference between colonists supporting a rebellion against English rule, and saying things that could be taken as a recommendation to overthrow *all* ruling governments...including the French monarchy.

"Being ruled by a king who is an ocean away means that his choices aren't always going to be in the best interest of all of his people," I said as I glanced at Alize and Celina. More than two hundred years, and even a government selected by the people still didn't command equal rights for *all* of its people. I continued, "Yes, what happens in the colonies will probably spread. And yes, it might cause some...unrest, but we can't allow the fear of what may happen to prevent us from doing what we know is right."

Alexandre studied me for a moment, then looked over at his daughter and the still-healing young woman next to her. "Others may not believe that the colonies have a chance of winning, but I do. And I believe that revolution will come to France as well. Because of my family's ties to royalty, I fear for my daughter's safety in the years to come."

"Papa," Alize started.

He smiled at her, a sad look in his eyes. "There are those who would want to take your happiness from you because they do not understand it. In society here, you are too visible, but in the colonies, you could be safe."

It hit me before the others, and I watched the realization dawning on their faces one by one.

"Papa, no!" Alize rattled something off in French, but I didn't need to understand the language to know that she was begging her father not to send her away.

"You want us to take Alize with us when we return," I said.

"She and Celina. I would consider it a great personal favor." He looked at his daughter. "I want you to take them somewhere they can be safe. Together."

Alize stifled a sob, and Celina put her arms around the other girl.

I glanced at Gracen to make sure we were on the same page, and he gave me a nod that spoke volumes.

"It wouldn't be a favor, Sir," I answered honestly. "Your daughter is the reason I'm alive today. And you have shown us such kindness by sheltering us here. We would only be repaying you the service of taking care of us. Of course we'll take them with us."

I felt as if I'd been waiting for days even though I knew I'd only arrived at the base hospital a couple of hours ago. I watched doctors and nurses shuffling back and forth, none of them bothering to look at me. The activity never seemed to slow down. The medic who'd come with me when we'd heard the news that James Dobkins was in critical condition had left some time ago. The charge nurse had already explained that there was a possibility that we wouldn't even be allowed to see James today and certainly not until he was stable. But, I'd wanted to wait. Needed to see him with my own eyes.

Shrapnel wounds, they'd said. I'd seen enough in my time in the service to know that those could range from minor injuries easily treated in the field, to fatal ones that wouldn't stand up to any doctoring, no matter who was doing it.

Still, I couldn't help but think that if I'd been

there, I could've done better. It was a shitty thing to think, I knew, but the thought was there, telling me that it would be my fault if James died.

Another doctor exited from the direction they'd taken James, but I didn't even look up. My cheek began to slide off of my palm as my head nodded with the suppressed urge to fall asleep. Dimly, I was considering heading to the cafeteria for a cup of very strong, black coffee when a voice spoke near me.

"Miss? Are you the one who's waiting for news on Private Dobkins?"

My head shot up to find the doctor standing only a few feet away from me.

I stood up quickly. "Yes. How is he?"

The doctor's expression was blank, and the nerves that had been bouncing around in my chest for the past half dozen hours turned into a knot, settling in the pit of my stomach.

"I'm sorry, but he didn't make it."

I stared at him, not believing the words I was hearing.

"One of his lungs was completely crushed, and a number of other vital organs were severely damaged in the crash as well. We kept him going as long as possible on a ventilator, hoping we might be able to pull him through if we could stabilize his pulse and repair the damage, but it was too much."

The walls felt as if they were closing in. If I'd been there, I could have saved him, I told myself. If only I'd been there. I could have saved him...

I jerked awake, releasing a short, harsh gasp. In a moment, strong arms were around me, Gracen's voice softly murmuring my name.

It had only been a dream, albeit one that had

been based in an excruciating reality.

Gracen pressed a kiss to my forehead. "Were you dreaming of that man?"

I shook my head. The feeling of helplessness, lack of control, I'd felt in both situations had been similar, but there had been no terror in my memory of my friend's death, only grief.

"You are safe," Gracen whispered. "You are here with me, and you are safe."

I was safe, and so were Alize and Celina. I was going to do for them what I hadn't been able to do for James. What I hadn't been able to do for Celina in that house. I refused to accept anything else. I would move heaven and earth to make them as safe as I was in my husband's arms.

"I love you." I pressed my face into his neck, inhaling his familiar scent, letting myself relax into him, letting him comfort me.

The worries would come, I knew, but for right now, this was enough.

Chapter 28

I remembered a time when a man from my unit had been shipped home, told that he'd done his duty, that his service to his country was over at the ripe age of twenty-five. I'd sent him back to the States knowing that most of the work had still been ahead of him. Physically, he'd had a hard road ahead, but the most challenging part, I'd known, would be the mental recovery that would take far longer than the healing of physical afflictions.

The same was true for Celina. She'd suffered bodily harm, but the emotional effects were far worse. I'd never dealt in the psychological side of things, but I hadn't made it through six years in the army without learning a thing or two, so I tended to her mind as well as her body as best I could as the days inched by.

Her fractured fingers had been stubborn to heal, but they were looking far better. Without traditional plaster for a cast, I'd fashioned a brace of sorts that kept her fingers immobile. I wasn't sure if her slow progress was due to the lack of a real cast or simply due to how much her malnourished body needed to repair.

"It's looking good," I said as I fastened the brace

in place again.

"Thank you, Madame." She gave me a soft smile.

Even without Alize around, smiling was finally becoming increasingly more familiar to Celina. Not that I could blame the girl for being skittish. Over the past couple weeks, I'd learned more about the life that she'd come from, and it had been enough to make me grateful that I'd been kidnapped so I could rescue her. What I'd endured at Harry's hand in those two days was nothing compared to what she'd been through.

After her father had borrowed money to feed his family, they'd been indebted to the couple who owned the boarding house where we'd been kept. After managing to owe far more money than they'd ever be able to repay, both of Celina's parents had passed away within two months of each other. Though they'd been doing whatever they could to keep Celina and her younger brother alive, it had meant she'd been left with life as an indentured servant or imprisonment as being her only options. To keep her brother alive, she'd essentially sold herself to the couple, supporting her brother from the age of thirteen until he also died.

Harry had abused Celina from the moment he'd taken up at the boarding house a few weeks ago, and the only time she'd gone to her masters, she'd been told to keep her mouth shut and do whatever Harry wanted of her. She didn't know what he did for a living, but he would leave for days at a time, then return and spend a few days hurting her before repeating the process. I didn't have to ask her to know that my presence had made it worse. Though there was nothing I could have done about it, I still felt somehow responsible.

"I would have died there if it had not been for you and Gracen." As she had before, Celina displayed an uncanny ability to read what I was thinking. "And it would have destroyed Alize."

Some may have dismissed that as romantic nonsense, but I saw how the two of them looked at each other, and I knew how I would have felt if I'd lost Gracen. As it was, I knew Harry's death was weighing heavily on Gracen's mind, despite everything he'd done. I reminded myself to tell him what Celina had said. Killing someone was never easy, especially when it wasn't during a battle. He'd done it in defense of Celina and me, and he needed to be reminded of that.

"Are you afraid?" Alize asked suddenly as she reached over and took Celina's uninjured hand. "Being a part of a war? Being a *woman* in war?"

I didn't need either of them to explain what they were really asking. After the brutality of what Celina had been through, after seeing women being essentially sold off to whoever their family felt would make the best husband, they knew how most men viewed and treated women. Unfortunately, ones like Alexandre and Gracen were the exception and not the rule...and even they didn't quite get it.

When I'd been tending to Celina's injuries, I'd also been building up her hopes, telling her how the fight for freedom would eventually reach women too. I knew that, sometimes, I spoke with far too much factual certainty, and I'd catch Celina and Alize staring at me. I knew I had to be careful, but when they asked questions like that, when I saw them fearing what the world would think of them, it was hard to couch knowledge of the future in vague terms that could be easily dismissed.

"It's not about being afraid," I said finally. "It's about doing what's right despite being afraid. And when something this big is on the line, it's definitely worth fighting through the fear."

"You truly believe that your people can defeat an army that the French have been unable to conquer?" Alize asked, more surprise than arrogance in her voice.

"I do," I said. "I believe that people who fight for their beliefs, who fight for their basic freedoms, are far stronger than most realize." I smiled at the two of them and continued, "And I truly believe that, one day, people will win the right to love whoever they want. It won't be easy, and the battles will be fought in much different ways, but it will happen."

The young women stared at me for several silent seconds, and I wondered if I'd gone too far.

"Are you a *mystique*?" Celina asked, her eyes wide with wonder. "Do you see the future?"

I thought of Dye and the things that she'd said, the way she'd almost seemed to know things that she shouldn't. Those might've been coincidences, but what I knew was fact. Though how I knew it, I supposed, was a bit on the mystical side. If there was a scientific explanation for it, I hadn't found it yet, and I doubted I ever would.

I wasn't sure how much I could tell them, but I went with what I could. "In a way."

Yeah, that was a good explanation.

"You are a strange woman, Honor Lightwood," Alize said but was looking at me so fondly, it took the edge off the words.

She had no idea.

As she and Celina walked away, I was struck by a memory.

"What are you doing?" I asked Rogers. I wasn't really interested in what he was doing. I just wanted to find anything that would take my mind off the nausea I'd been experiencing the last couple days. For some reason, adjusting to the heat this time had made me sick to my stomach.

"Updating my will," he answered, not looking up from the page.

I propped myself up on one elbow, but quickly rested my cheek against my outstretched arm again when the world spun. "Why? What's changed? Don't tell me you won the lottery and have a bunch of extra cash to dole out," I teased.

Rogers, however, didn't laugh. "I found out that my house is worth more than it used to be due to real estate in the area and the extensions that've been added. I need to make sure my mom gets all of it."

"I thought she was already getting everything."

"The law is picky," he said. "It needs to be said just right and clearly."

"You're still giving me your Mustang, right?"

A slight smile worked its way onto Rogers's lips. "Not a chance in hell. You'd run it into the ground."

I chuckled, but the sound had a somber note to it that I couldn't quite stop. "You're not planning on dying, are you? Because, I'll have you know that I won't allow it. I mean, we agreed that we were going to outlive each other."

Rogers glanced up at me, but the fact that he didn't even crack a smile told me that he was serious.

We all knew that death was something we faced on a daily basis here and that we needed to be *prepared for it at all times, but I didn't like talking about it, especially not like this. Not in this sort of rational manner. I wanted these men to go home after this was all over, raise families, pursue their civilian dreams. Every time we set foot on dangerous territory, I was praying that I wouldn't end up attending their funerals. I'd already gone to more than my fair share.*

"I don't like when you talk like that," I admitted. We rarely had heart-to-hearts, but when Rogers started to talk like this, I knew it was time to break that habit.

He sighed and looked up at me, his dark eyes meeting mine. "I appreciate what you're trying to do, Honor, but we both know the risks of our job."

I fiddled with the corner of the pillowcase beneath my head, my eyes on my short nails. I'd had to cut them to stop myself from nervously chewing on them. "It doesn't hurt to remain positive."

Rogers smiled, raising his eyebrows. "You're really going to give me that 'be positive' shit."

I rolled my eyes. "Of course not. I'm just saying."

"'Just saying' doesn't mean shit when you got insurgents shooting at you and trying to blow you up."

"Shut up and write your will already." I groaned as my stomach did another flip. It was going to be a long night.

"Madame Lightwood?" Celina's voice pulled me back, and I gave her a tight smile.

"I'm okay," I insisted. "Just thinking." I stood. "We should go get ready for dinner."

The girls agreed and hurried off.

For the first time since arriving here, I found myself genuinely wondering what was going on in my time. Would everyone think I'd simply vanished? I assumed my car had crashed, but there was no body for them to find. Would they suspect foul play? Would they accuse Bruce?

Shit.

I closed my eyes, rubbing my temples to try to stave off the headache that was throbbing at the base of my skull.

"The revolution is on everyone's minds, I think."

I opened my eyes as Gracen came toward me. He wrapped his arms around me, kissing me on my forehead before pulling me toward him. I didn't tell him I wasn't thinking about the war just then. It would only make him think that I was regretting my decision. I wasn't.

I leaned against him, letting the steady beat of his heart turn my mind back to the here and now. It wasn't all bad. Christmas was in a few days, and we were safe here. We had work to do, true, but that didn't mean we couldn't take a few minutes for ourselves. I had a feeling, with what was coming, we'd need it.

Chapter 29

"I wish my father had not decided to host a party this year," Alize said with a sigh.

Alexandre had made the announcement that his annual Christmas Eve ball was still officially on, then thrown himself into preparations. I had a feeling he was trying to keep himself from thinking about Alize leaving, and I understood his desire to put aside unpleasant thoughts with things that were nicer to think about.

"Why not?" I asked, curious about her response to her father's announcement that it was time for us to dress for the ball.

"If this is to be my last..." Her voice cracked. "I want...*passer la Noël en famille*." She shook her head, and I could see her eyes shining with tears.

"You will be with your father again," Celina insisted, putting her hands on Alize's shoulders. "This will not be your final *Noël* with him."

"She's right," I said. "He just wants you to be safe."

Alize chuckled, a harsh, bitter sound. "Yes. Safe, by leaving. By running away to the colonies. By leaving everyone I know and love."

"Everyone?" Celina's voice was soft, but it did

what no argument on my part would've been able to accomplish.

It got Alize's attention. She turned toward Celina, taking the young woman's hands in her own.

"No, no, *mon amour*." Alize brushed her lips across Celina's. "Not everyone. Not as long as I have you. But am I wrong for not wanting to lose my home?"

"Staying here could get you and the woman you love killed." I hated having to be so blunt, but I knew it was probably the only thing that would get through to her.

Alize paled, and I second-guessed my words, but only for a moment. Perhaps she needed to be scared into realizing that even though the prospect of traveling overseas was scary, her greatest fears were far more likely to become a reality if she remained in France.

"Please, do not say that," Alize murmured.

"I have to," I said, forcing my voice to stay gentle. "What lies ahead will most likely be uncomfortable for you, and much different than what you've experienced in the past, but you have a better chance of staying safe with Gracen and me than you do here."

"Gracen and Honor are good people," Celina said. "We need to trust them."

Alize nodded and allowed Celina to embrace her. I smiled at them both as I slipped into the hall and headed down the hall to my room. I needed to get ready, and I wasn't looking forward to having to pile on all the layers. Especially the whole corset thing.

Just the thought made my stomach roll.

As soon as I came into the bedroom, I went

straight to the bed and laid down, rolling onto my back. I stared up at the ceiling and took a deep breath, willing the nausea to pass. French food and anxiety weren't a good mix.

"Honor," Gracen spoke as the door opened. "Are you alright?"

"Yeah," I said, swallowing, hoping I wouldn't have to make a run for the wash basin.

He suddenly appeared, looking down at me. "Are you certain? You look as if you are going to—"

I jumped up, making it to the nearby basin just in time. He came behind me almost immediately, gathering my hair away from my face as I spit out the bile filling my mouth. Once I was sure I was done, I rinsed and then turned to my husband with a sigh.

"How bad would it be if I used the stomach flu as an excuse to stay up here all night?" I groaned.

He made a sympathetic sound as he put his arm around my waist and led me back to the bed. "You do what you need to do, my love. You must take care of yourself."

I felt a twinge of guilt as I considered crawling under the blankets and staying there all night. Then I shook it off and reminded myself why I was here, why I'd come to France with my husband.

So I got up and filled a fresh basin with water as Gracen carried the other basin out of the room. By the time he returned, I was almost completely dressed, and the nausea in my stomach had settled. I took the rest of the time I needed to gather myself and was able to smile when Gracen held out his hand to me.

The two of us made our way downstairs, ready to continue to schmooze and smile and pretend that everything was okay.

The party appeared to be a success almost from moment one. Nearly forty people, none of whom we had to worry about betraying us to the English. And all of them already laughing and joking.

It should have been calming, to finally be able to relax. Knowing that everyone here had the same political agenda. I could see Celina coaxing Alize into enjoying herself, even if only a little.

None of them, however, had the same things at stake as Gracen and I did.

"Do you see the three over by the balcony doors?" Alexandre asked as we waited for dinner to be called.

Gracen nodded.

"They are prepared to discuss stronghold provisions, as well as possibilities for evading any blockages the British navy sets up."

I surveyed the group of men, hoping that I wasn't being too obvious. Two of them looked just like the rest of the room's occupants: stylishly dressed peacocks, enjoying their high stations in an opulent setting. I could only hope there was more grit than met the eye beneath those stuffy waistcoats and aristocratic gestures. Then again, it wasn't as if they themselves would be running blockades. They would be supplying the much-needed money from the safety of their homes.

My attention, however, lingered on the third man. It took a few moments for me to place the reasons he stood out to me since his clothing, while not quite as impressive as his companions, still showed wealth. Possessing an air of superiority was by no means a novelty in this place, but this man's aloofness seemed drastically exaggerated somehow.

He wasn't doing much talking, his dark eyes sharp as they scanned the room. When they landed on me, I barely suppressed a shiver, my instincts screaming at me to stay away from him. But I had a job to do. Besides, he was far from the first man to give me the creeps.

Alexandre, Gracen, and I made our way over, my tension increasing with each step. The hairs on the back of my neck stood up, but I forced a smile.

"Monsieurs," Alexandre greeted them warmly, and the men nodded in acknowledgment. "May I present Gracen and Honor Lightwood, visiting us from the American colonies. Gracen and Honor, Gulliory, Bellamy, and Faver."

Faver, he was the suspicious one. He remained silent except for a polite, heavily accented greeting, but I still couldn't shake the feeling that he was up to something. I didn't want to come out and accuse any of Alexandre's guests, but every soldier's instinct I had told me that this was not a good man. He had almost feminine-looking features, a generous mouth, the sort of features that would eventually be referred to as a "baby face." It didn't do anything to lessen the edge I felt.

"There are a number of things that I wish to discuss with you gentlemen," Gracen began.

For the first time, it didn't bother me that Gracen was the one who had to take the lead, even though I was the one with knowledge of the future. These men wouldn't listen to me, so I'd use that to my advantage, observe without really being seen.

To my disappointment, I couldn't find anything of note about Faver, and certainly nothing that would explain the warning signals I kept getting. When we moved on, I tried to push my concerns away, dismissing them as paranoia brought on by my kidnapping, but I could feel Faver watching me as I walked. Drawing Gracen's attention to it when I had no proof wouldn't do any good.

Still, the problem gnawed at me through the entire dinner, and afterward as everyone gathered in the ballroom. By then, my head was pounding and my stomach churning. While it was cold outside, the press of bodies in the room made it unbelievably stifling, which did nothing to help the cloying mixture of perfumes and body odor. I hadn't been there for more than a few minutes before I excused myself. If I didn't get some fresh air, I was going to be sick.

I was halfway down the corridor before my stomach started to calm. Breathing was easier out here, but the constricting corset I wore still made it relatively difficult. Not for the first time, I found myself longing for a comfortable pair of jeans. I would've even taken one of those annoying strapless bras that I hated.

"It is a nice night for a stroll, is it not, Madame Lightwood?"

I stiffened, hoping that the strange voice belonged to one of the other two dozen men rather than the one my gut was telling me. I turned slowly, giving myself enough time to make my face a cordial mask.

"Monsieur Faver, correct?"

He nodded once, his eyes remaining on my face.

"It is indeed a lovely night." I glanced behind him on the off chance I'd see someone else coming this way, but the hallway was empty. "I was just taking some air before heading back in to find my husband."

"Ah, yes, your husband."

I didn't care for the way he said the word, or how one side of his mouth twisted into a grimace of a smile.

"Monsieur Lightwood has quite a lot to say about the American colonies."

"He does," I agreed. "And we would both be happy to speak with you at greater length regarding your take on things."

My mind raced. Faver hadn't done anything aggressive, but all sorts of warning bells were going off in my head, adrenaline flooding my system. I needed to get where there were more people.

"Is that so?" The tone was tinged with a mockery that made my mouth go dry.

I remembered reading somewhere that some famous serial killer – Bundy or Dahmer maybe – had the sort of soft features that made people trust them. Faver, I thought, was like that.

"Of course." My cheeks were starting to hurt with the force of my smile. "Will you excuse me? My husband will be worrying about me."

Faver inclined his head and took half a step to the side. It wasn't enough for me to pass by without brushing up against him, but he was no longer completely blocking my way either. I'd take what I could get though.

I was right next to him when his hand shot out and closed around my upper arm. I gave him a cold look as my pulse began to race, but he didn't acknowledge it.

"Shall we go somewhere more private to have our discussion, Madame Lightwood?"

"No." The word came out small. I shook my head and pulled myself up straighter. "Let me go,

Monsieur Faver."

"I do not think my employer would want me to do that," he said. He pushed open the door next and dragged me after him.

I was almost completely inside when my paralysis broke, and I started to struggle. I almost managed to pull myself free when Faver's hand cracked against my cheek.

"Bastard!" I shouted as I used my free hand to strike him. The angle was bad, and I only managed to catch his shoulder. "Help!"

Faver clamped a hand over my mouth and pulled me backwards, kicking the door closed behind him. "The music in the ballroom is too loud for anyone to hear you."

My heart sank as I realized he was right. I'd walked too far away. Unless someone was looking for me, I was in this alone. I needed to keep my head together.

"If I remove my hand, will you stay quiet?"

I nodded. I didn't have enough mobility in this dress to properly use the hand-to-hand combat skills I possessed, so I needed to take him off-guard, and to do that, I had to earn some trust. He let go of me and took a step back, keeping himself between me and the door.

The room wasn't lit, but the moonlight shining through the window was bright enough that I could see. We were in a sitting room of some kind, a room I'd only vaguely registered during my time here. Chairs, a sofa, some books. Nothing that looked like it would be of any use to me.

Then I saw the fireplace.

And the metal poker leaning against it.

Jackpot.

"My husband doesn't have any money here," I said as I inched sideways. I'd likely only have one shot at this. "I'm not sure what sort of ransom you think you'll get for me."

Faver laughed, a genuinely amused sound that scared me worse than his silence would have. "I already have my payment guaranteed. And with Monsieur Pasternak deceased, I shall be able to keep it all for myself."

A cold knot settled in my stomach. Pasternak. That was the last name of the man who'd kidnapped me. The man Gracen had killed.

"You paid him to torture me?"

Faver shrugged. "My employer had hoped that such an attack could be attributed to political goals and would achieve the desired result."

I took another sidestep. "What desired result? Me dead?"

"Dead or ruined, my employer was not...picky. Only that it would result in Monsieur Lightwood returning to the colonies on the right side of the conflict."

The suspicion hit me hard enough to make me gasp. I didn't want to believe it, and I definitely didn't want to ask it, but I knew that unless I did, it would always be a possibility in my mind.

"Who is your employer?" Another sidestep, and I was close enough to lunge for the poker.

"Monsieur Lightwood." Faver smiled as he cut the distance between us in half. "The elder, of course."

A punch to the gut couldn't have affected me more at that moment. "He hates me that much?" The question came out in a whisper.

"I was to be the middle man," Faver said,

ignoring me. He almost sounded like he was talking to himself, psyching himself up to do what needed to be done. "But when your husband killed Harry, I knew I needed to get my hands dirty. At first, the idea was distasteful, but I am beginning to see the appeal."

I yanked my thoughts back to the present. I'd deal with the ramifications of what I just learned once I was safe. As Faver came toward me, I knew I was out of time. I dove for the fireplace, my fingers closing around the handle of the poker just as Faver grabbed for me. He caught my sleeve, the fabric digging into my arm as he pulled.

Every summer growing up, my family had gone to picnics held at whatever base we happened to be, and inevitably, my father and brother would get a baseball game going. While I'd never been good enough to play on an organized team, I'd always enjoyed it. It had been nearly ten years since the last time I'd played, but I called up everything I ever learned as I swung the poker straight at Faver's head.

Metal met bone with a sickening crunch, and I watched Faver's eyes widen in surprise for two long seconds. Then he dropped to the ground, dead or unconscious, I didn't know. That didn't matter. I didn't plan to stick around to check. I needed to get out of here, needed to find Gracen and tell him what happened.

I just didn't know how to tell him that his father had tried to have me killed.

Chapter 30

I opened my eyes, and the room swam into focus. The thought that it was Christmas Day came up almost immediately, but it didn't bring with it any of the usual joy I'd felt in the past.

Actually, I realized, it had been a while since I'd been happy on Christmas morning. The last two years, I'd been on tour. The year before that, Bruce had thrown a fit that I'd wanted to spend all day with my family rather than in bed with him, so that had cast a damper on the whole thing.

"Merry Christmas, my love."

His voice reminded me that I did have something to look forward to today, and I rolled over to face him.

"Merry Christmas."

He reached over and brushed the back of his hand down my cheek. "Are you all right?"

I nodded. After I'd gotten away from Faver, I'd found Gracen and Alexandre. Things became a bit of a blur after that. Faver had been arrested, and Alexandre apologetic. I'd never seen St. James so furious. He'd dressed down his guards so thoroughly that I hadn't needed to know French to know he'd been pissed. He'd apologized over and over until Alize had finally managed to get him to stop.

The party had ended, but my night hadn't been over yet. I'd had to tell Gracen what Faver had said about Roston. It wasn't a pleasant conversation, though it had been pretty much one-sided. Gracen had just listened, his face growing paler by the second. When I finished, he'd taken me in his arms, brought me upstairs. We hadn't spoken as we'd gotten ready for bed, but now that we were awake, I wondered if we were going to talk about it.

Pain was evident in Gracen's eyes. "I keep wondering what I could have done. To prevent it..."

"You could have left me," I whispered. "We both know that the only thing your father would accept is you marrying Clara and supporting the British."

"Never." His voice was earnest. He leaned over and kissed my forehead. "I hate what he did, but I will *not* let him take you from me."

I slid my hand over Gracen's chest, moving in closer as he pulled me to him. His heart thudded against my palm, a steady rhythm that grounded me. His hands slid down my back to cup my ass, and I let out a laugh as he rolled us over.

"I love you, Honor Lightwood," he said, his smile settling into something a bit more serious. He sat up, his hands sliding down to ease my legs around his waist.

"I love you too." I wrapped my arms around his neck, making a small noise in the back of my throat as my breasts pressed against his chest, the friction making my nipples harden.

He wrapped his hand around the back of my neck, pulling until our mouths met. Heat spread down through my body, tightening things low inside me. I could feel him hardening against me, our bodies separated by the thin fabric of our nightshirts.

"I want you inside me," I murmured against his mouth. "Need to feel you stretching me so wide around you. Filling me up. Please, baby."

Gracen made a growling sound as he reached between us, his fingers jerking our clothes out of the way. His eyes locked with mine, deep and full of all the things that we weren't saying. I let out a cry as he pulled me down, burying himself inside me with one thrust. I dug my nails into his arms, a soft whimper escaping. It didn't matter how many times or ways we did this, that first moment he slid inside me was always overwhelming.

"My beautiful wife." His voice was rough, but his touch was gentle as he cupped my chin and guided my mouth back to his.

As we moved, heat built between us, chasing away the chill in the room. Chasing away everything but the feel of him. His scent. The sound of our breathing. Every sense was filled with him and us. I clung to him, kissing my way down his neck, the salt from his skin bitter on my tongue. His teeth and lips worked over my own throat, and I was dimly aware that we were both leaving marks, but I didn't care. A part of me even liked the idea of making sure everyone could see that he was mine and I was his.

"I cannot..." A shudder ran through him. "I...Honor, my love."

"I know." I tightened around him. "Let go."

My name came out of his mouth like a combination curse and prayer as he came. A rush of heat filled me, and I ground down on him, rotating my hips to get that extra friction I needed to send me over the edge.

"Ahh..." The sound was half-moan, half-shout,

but all I felt was pleasure. Everything went white, and a small part of my mind recognized the humor in a whole different sort of white Christmas.

We'd have today, I decided. One day where it could just be about us. It was, after all, our first Christmas together.

"I think that should be a Christmas tradition," I said as I ran my fingers through his soft hair. "Best way to wake up ever."

He chuckled, the rumble a gentle vibration against my chest, his breath hot against my neck. "I agree."

We stayed joined a while longer before we finally stretched out next to each other. He ran his fingers up my arm, tracing patterns on my bare skin, each touch sending little sparkles of electricity through me.

"You know," he said. "I was thinking. We may need for you to step into a more masculine role when we return to Boston. You can wear men's clothes the way you did when we first met, an open disguise."

"You want me to dress as a man?"

"It might be a good idea."

I sighed. "It might have been, but I'm afraid that'll be quite impossible now."

Gracen pulled back, looking at me in confusion. "I do not understand. You suggested it to Washington yourself."

"I did," I said, knowing it was time to tell him what I'd guessed only a couple days ago. "It's just that I won't be able to look the part soon...not once I start to show anyway." I gave him a weak smile. "Merry Christmas?"

Our relationship finally seemed to be on the

right track again, but adding another person to the equation, not to mention a helpless, innocent one, would change everything. Though I didn't yet know if it would be a good change or a bad one. Being pregnant would keep anyone from being suspicious, no doubt, but I was certain no one was going to let me help in that condition, and that wasn't just an opinion from this time period. I just didn't want anyone to see me as helpless, or my child as a burden.

Gracen stared at me, his eyes wide. Expression unreadable.

Finally, he released a soft chuckle, resting his forehead on my breast. "Damn," he murmured.

"Are you upset?" I asked, squeezing his shoulder with my fingers, my heart in my throat.

He looked up at me, cupping my cheek in his hand. "Upset? Of course not. You are going to have my baby."

The wonder in his tone brought tears to my eyes, and my vision blurred for a few moments before I brushed the drops away. When I could see clearly again, I found a shadow in Gracen's eyes.

"What's wrong?"

"I cannot help but think…" The words trailed off. He took my hand and kissed my palm.

"Think what?"

"That you would rather be in your time, with your family, at a time like this."

My heart twisted painfully, and it was my turn to rest my hand on his cheek. I leaned over and give him a soft kiss.

"*You* are my family, Gracen Lightwood." My words were firm, certain. "You and this baby are my family. Do I wish my parents and brother could meet our child? Yes. But if I had to choose, I would choose you and this baby over everything that other time has to offer."

He laced his fingers between mine. "Are you certain?"

I squeezed his hand. "I *did* choose you, remember?"

A wide smile broke out across his face as he grabbed me, rolling us over so that I was on my back. He propped himself up over me, kissed the tip of my nose, and then moved down my body, tugging at my nightshirt as he went. I yanked it over my head, but before I could process round two, I realized that he wasn't initiating sex.

He was...*communing* with the baby. It was the only word I could think of that even came close to describing the look of awe and love on his face. He touched my stomach lightly, almost reverently. When he lightly kissed just below my bellybutton, everything inside me shifted, and I found that I could love him even more than I already did.

"Hello, my little one."

His voice grew softer until I couldn't hear what else he was saying. That was okay though. He wasn't talking to me. I smiled, reaching down to comb my fingers through his hair as his lips moved against my skin. I didn't know everything about what the future held, but this moment, right here, right now, I was content.

The End

The Lightwood Affair continues in the final book Love and Honor (The Lightwood Affair Book 3)

More from M.S. Parker

Fire and Honor
Make Me Yours
The Billionaire's Sub
The Billionaire's Mistress
Con Man
HERO
A Legal Affair
The Client
Indecent Encounter
Dom X
Unlawful Attraction
Chasing Perfection
Blindfold

Club Prive
The Pleasure Series
Exotic Desires
Pure Lust

Casual Encounter
Sinful Desires

Twisted Affair
Serving HIM

Acknowledgement

First, I would like to thank all my readers. Without you, my books would not exist. I truly appreciate each and every one of you.

A big "thanks" goes out to all the Facebook fans, street team, beta readers, and advanced reviewers. You are a HUGE part of the success of the series.

I must thank my PA, Shannon Hunt. Without you my life would be a complete and utter mess. Also, a big "THANK YOU" goes out to my editor Lynette and my wonderful cover designer, Sinisa. You make my ideas and writing look so good.

About the Author

M. S. Parker is a USA Today Bestselling author and the author of the Erotic Romance series, Club Privè and Chasing Perfection.

Living in Las Vegas, she enjoys sitting by the pool with her laptop writing on her next spicy romance.

Growing up all she wanted to be was a dancer, actor or author. So far only the latter has come true but M. S. Parker hasn't retired her dancing shoes just yet. She is still waiting for the call for her to appear on Dancing With The Stars.

When M. S. isn't writing, she can usually be found reading– oops, scratch that! She is always writing.

Made in United States
North Haven, CT
30 August 2023